REST IN PIECES

"Okay, boys, stand these trespassers alongside buryin' holes," Queeg commanded. "Six o' you form a firin' squad. Get your minds off whiskey and women long enough to hold a bead."

"Your boss's going to be mighty sore about this when he hears the news," Jessie said.

Queeg gave another of his maniacal snickers. "So far as my boss is concerned, you're gonna be a dead issue."

"Ready!

"Take aim!"

Jessie stiffened. She clamped her teeth to keep from screaming, her lips moving stiffly as she whispered a prayer. . . .

— WESLEY ELLIS —

LONE STAR

IN THE DEVIL'S PLAYGROUND

JOVE BOOKS, NEW YORK

LONE STAR IN THE DEVIL'S PLAYGROUND

A Jove Book / published by arrangement with
the author

PRINTING HISTORY
Jove edition / June 1991

ISBN: 0-515-10598-8

Jove Books are published by The Berkley Publishing Group,
200 Madison Avenue, New York, New York 10016.
The name "JOVE" and the "J" logo
are trademarks belonging to Jove Publications, Inc.

10 9 8 7 6 5 4 3 2 1

LONE STAR

IN THE
DEVIL'S PLAYGROUND

★

Chapter 1

This region of high prairie desert was called the Devil's Playground, and traveling through it, Jessica Starbuck understood why. It was a country of chasms and gulches and ravines, of lonesome monoliths and rolling pumice flows, and, in the distance, sometimes, in the chilly spring sun, sawtooth buttes of gray granite, like sentinels. It made her frigid and forlorn just to look at the brutal, bleak expanse stretching about her.

Outwardly Jessie and her companion, Ki, appeared to be weary riders slumped in their saddles, unaware of their surroundings, and uncaring. And in keeping with this guise, as well as for comfort, both wore well-worn jeans and denim jackets, dusty woolen shirts and sweat-stained, flop-brimmed hats. Jessie did not appear to be what she really was—a proud, aristocratic woman in her mid-twenties; a crack shot with her now-holstered pistol or the twin-shot derringer concealed behind her wide belt buckle; and a shrewd, knowledgeable heiress to immense wealth,

1

the Starbuck international business empire. Nor did Ki seem to be more than a tall, lean man in his early thirties, of mixed Japanese and Caucasian blood, and so peaceful by nature that he lacked a gunbelt or any other sign of a firearm. In fact, though, he was a samurai-trained master of martial arts, in whose old leather vest were secreted short daggers and similar small throwing weapons, including razor-edged, star-shaped steel disks called *shuriken*.

In truth, they rode warily, for any stranger in this wild country could well be an outlaw. Remaining carefully alert was difficult, for they had ridden steadily for two hundred miles from Elko, Nevada, the nearest rail stop, after an interminable trip by train and stage from Jessie's Circle Star Ranch in Texas. They'd had to buy their horses and gear, since Elko liveries insisted rental nags be returned in short order, but fortunately they'd found a tough, sturdy pinto mare for Jessie and a deep-brisketed sorrel gelding for Ki. Then, heading northwesterly, they had crossed the Independence Mountains and followed the South Fork, Owyhee River out of Nevada into the Territory of Idaho. Initially the Idaho terrain hadn't seemed too remarkable, merely stark, but after they cut west from the Owyhee, it became outlandish: patches of pine and gorse and grass, but mainly bare, ruddy-dun hardpan, the vegetation scraggly and scattered.

Equally outlandish was the reason for their arduous journey. Last January, a storm-delayed Christmas card, addressed to Jessie, had arrived

2

at Starbuck headquarters on her ranch. Along with the printed, rather syrupy season's greetings was a handwritten, strangely cryptic message:

If you would be willing to contribute your personal services and good offices on a venture of national importance, please advise when you can visit me. I will contact you in Beyond and you will recognize me by the sheepskin headband I shall be wearing. Take care.
Y'r m'st ob'd'nt s'rv'nt,
Winthrop Folgeron
Triad Ranch, Beyond, Idaho Terr.

Even if Jessie had understood what lay behind Winthrop Folgeron's puzzling message—which she hadn't—she wouldn't have been able to respond right away. The winter had proven to be a howlin' bitch, one blizzard after another sweeping the Sierras, Midwest and central Texas. It had been sheer luck that his Christmas card had made it through at all. Lengthy travel had been simply too hazardous for more than the most extreme emergencies—which this hadn't appeared to be; after all, Folgeron had mentioned caution but not urgency, and had mailed rather than wired his appeal—so Jessie hadn't felt obliged to act until spring thaw.

Yet there hadn't been much question about going. Although Jessie didn't know Folgeron personally, had never met the man, she'd certainly heard of him. Winthrop Folgeron was one of America's foremost photographers, renowned for his battle pictures of

3

the Civil War, then afterward for his portraiture of Indian peoples commissioned by the Department of the Interior. Now retired from his position as official photographer for the government agency, he was living his elder years as something of a recluse, out in the middle of nowhere.

Out nowhere was putting it mildly. The map Jessie had consulted showed the section bald as an onion—the unsurveyed Devil's Playground, where the south corners of Oregon and Idaho joined at the Nevada line. No mountains, rivers, trails or settlements were indicated. Not even Beyond, the town closest to Folgeron's Triad Ranch.

But however strange, however remote, a summons for help from someone as prominent as Winthrop Folgeron could not be taken lightly. Particularly when he had requested her personally, and had spoken of national importance. And Jessie took such responsibilities seriously, controlling her huge inheritance and far-flung interests with acumen and strength, harder than a keg of railroad spikes if need be. To her way of thinking, it was almost her duty to go.

Besides, Jessie was curious.

So once the weather had turned, Jessie had sent word to Folgeron that they were coming, then set off for Beyond, accompanied as always by Ki, her confidant and protector. Originally, many years back, when Ki had emigrated from Japan to San Francisco, the black-haired, almond-eyed, bronze-complected man had been hired by Jessie's father. Consequently, he and Jessie had virtually grown up

4

together, and after Alex Starbuck was murdered, it seemed only fitting for them to continue together. As affectionate and trusting as any blood brother and sister, they made a formidable team.

Now, just after sunset, in the slate gray of early night, Ki surveyed the dark scatteration of hills and rolling desert. And sighed wearily. "That hostler in Elko who gave us directions," he recalled, "spoke of a place called Halfway Inn. We must be getting near it. Why don't we put up for the night there?"

Jessie made a "humph" sound, and tucked a stray wisp of coppery blond hair up under her hat. Ki wasn't fooling her; his suggestion was for her benefit, not because he was so bone tired, but she wasn't about to let him patronize her. She cast him a sharp glance, and despite an expression mirroring the exhausting effects of their long journey, the spring chill could not dampen the warmth of her sultry face, with its high cheekbones, audacious green eyes and the provocative quirk of her lips. "The man likewise said we could reach Beyond by daylight," she retorted.

"Well, at least we might take a break just ahead," Ki suggested, pointing to where the trail skirted a nester's abandoned farmstead on their left.

There were two dilapidated structures—a shack set up facing the trail, and a barn at its rear—at right angles, forming a kind of broken-linked L. They sat back a short ways in a field whose earth had once been broken by the nester's plow, then left to the tumbleweeds. In the crotch of the L was what had caught Ki's attention—a rock-walled well topped by a creaky wooden windlass, from which an

5

old wooden bucket hung by a saddle rope.

Jessie viewed the stead with a different eye. As they walked their mounts off-trail toward the buildings, relaxed in their saddles, she murmured, "What a wonderful spot for a cross fire. Let's get our drink and go."

The fact that the rope and bucket were still in one piece indicated that long after the nester had pulled roots, wayfarers had been stopping by to quench their thirst. There was an unwritten law about such things, that when a rider had drunk his fill and watered his horse, he should lower the bucket back into the water to keep the sun from warping it. But the bucket now lay on the ground. It had not been exposed to the weather long enough for the wooden staves to warp and crack apart, and indeed, when Ki lifted the bucket, he noticed there was still a little moisture trapped at the bottom.

Ignoring his sorrel as it nudged his back, begging for water, Ki dunked the bucket deep into the well and let it soak for a while before cranking it to the surface. Only when the horses had drunk did Ki lower the bucket and draw it up to wash the dust from his and Jessie's throats. They took little sips, swallowing slowly, for the water had a bitter taste like quinine and soda, but it was harmless unless one over-drank. The Shoshone and Paiute claimed the bitter taste helped quench thirst far more effectively than clear water.

Ki had taken the bucket away from the horses before they had drunk too much and suffered the bloats. But their thirsts were not half-quenched yet, and they nickered for more. Dropping the bucket, Ki spun and headed for the barn, Jessie a pace behind. They had heard three horses and that was one too many.

Cautiously they entered the barn. Inside it was like a dusty wooden cave, tumbledown, hung with cobwebs, reeking of acrid old chaff and dung. A row of stalls and mangers along one side were partly demolished, used by somebody a long time ago for firewood, probably. No harness of any sort hung from the pegs around the walls, but just inside the double-doored entrance, Ki found a discarded candle stub melted to the center of a pie tin. Lighting the candle, Ki held the tin aloft and Jessie drew her pistol, and they studied the horse tied to a half-fallen rafter at the far end of the barn. All about them, beyond the reaches of the candle shine, lay impenetrable black shadows.

The horse, a shaggy, jerky-tough roan, appeared to have been run hard. Jessie wondered aloud if it had come from Beyond or Halfway Inn, and decided no. As Ki pointed out, the roan didn't have the look of a village horse; it was a range horse and was equipped, saddle gear and all, including emergency canteens and a Winchester .44–40 carbine in a saddle boot. That left the rider unaccounted for, possibly right here, right now, maybe even watching.

Ki called out, "If you don't start nothing, we won't."

There was no reply.

Moving warily, leaving Jessie to cover him, Ki began to look around.

7

He found the missing rider in one of the stalls, supine on the crusty ground. Joining Ki, Jessie estimated the man to be about thirty, but it was hard to tell, for sun and wind and several days' growth of brown beard stubble marked his features. He was clad in a linsey-woolsey shirt, a flannel-lined twill jumper which he had buttoned against the cold, and black woolen trousers thrust into the tops of scuffed black boots. The gun in the holster at his right hip was a .44–40 Colt Frontier revolver with a seven-and-a-half-inch barrel, and across his muscular chest was slung a "prairie" cartridge bandolier lined with cartridges. One arm was above his head. There were heel gouges in the ground by his boots. His hat, assuming he'd worn one, was gone, and there was a big wet blotch of blood making a sticky mess of his dark chestnut hair.

"Grazed by a bullet," Jessie said, hunkering down to examine the head wound. "He's sliced pretty deep. Likely a concussion, too. Can you get me some water and something to clean him up with?"

Going to the roan, Ki fetched a canteen and a spare shirt from the man's saddlebags. "Reckon he was shot outside, dragged in and left for dead," he surmised, returning. "But not by a robber. I didn't notice any money in his bags, but guns and saddles and a good horse are of value hereabouts."

Jessie swabbed the dirt from the wound as much as possible, hindered by the poor light and cold water. The man opened his eyes, looked at her unseeingly, and closed them again. The blood flow had almost stopped, in a jellylike coagulation, but she hastened the clotting by applying a handful of cobwebs, one of her grandfather's favorite old remedies. Her grandfather had also used horse dung, but Jessie passed that one up, binding the man's head with strips from his shirt.

"There's a chance. There's still life in him," she judged, sounding none too sure. "Help me get him into his saddle."

Ki nodded. "Now we sure enough have to stop at Halfway Inn."

★

Chapter 2

The night grew thick, with clouds in sooty patches and deep cobalt showing beyond. A cold, pallid moon was arcing toward midnight when Jessie and Ki finally came upon Halfway Inn, tucked in a hollow where their path intersected a couple of other lightly traveled, meandering trails at a water hole. Slopes of sagebrush and gnarled conifers ringed the hollow, and clumps of cottonwood grew along the bottom, shading the spring and adjacent Halfway Inn. A blocky, two-storied building of stone and log, the inn loomed dark and silent, vaguely sinister in the faint moon glow.

The spring was boxed in, with an old plank trough to siphon off the overflow. There, at a handy tie rack, they tethered their horses and the roan, which Ki had been leading by its reins. Then supporting the wounded man between them, they crossed to the inn and rapped loudly on its black, heavy oak front door. Chiseled in the stone cornice above the door was the legend *This portal is never barred to those who seek solace.*

"Smacks of a way station for outlaws and renegades," Jessie grumped as they waited.

A light appeared, through the grimy front window and chinks in the logs, and the door creaked open on iron hinges. On the threshold stood a pudgy, greasy, hog-jowled man wearing a bartender's apron around his neck like a bib. In his left hand was a bull's-eye lantern; in his right hand was a wicked looking .45 at full cock.

Gruff-voiced, he demanded, "Whatcher want?"

"A bed for this gent," Ki answered.

After an interminable pause, flashing the lantern in their faces, the proprietor stepped back a pace. " 'Aw' ri', foller me."

Traipsing after him, Jessie and Ki carried the comatose man down a short hallway and through the dimness of the main tavern room. Shadowy outlines could be seen of a crude bar of raw pine along one side, and a row of tables with soap boxes for chairs against the opposite wall. The proprietor then led them up a steep flight of stairs to the second floor, along a narrow corridor, and ushered them into a room. It was a miserable room, barely a notch above a hovel, with a swaybacked bed, warped bureau, and a rickety chair.

While the proprietor fumbled a kerosene lamp alight, Jessie and Ki pulled the bed covers open and laid the man on the mattress.

"Wouldn't happen to be a doctor under the roof?" Jessie asked.

The proprietor shook his head. "Nope, nearest sawbones is in Beyond, on down the trail."

"In that case, rustle up some hot water, soap and any medicants you might have on hand," Jessie instructed, and handed the proprietor a silver dollar.

Biting the dollar to make sure it was genuine, the proprietor grudgingly departed. Ki tugged at the man's boots and got them off, and it was when Ki was placing the boots upon the floor that the man once more raised his eyelids. He tried to sit up, but Jessie stopped him, gently.

"I don't know you," the man slurred.

"Easy, now. You're safe." Jessie introduced herself and Ki, adding that they had found him at the deserted homestead and brought him to Halfway Inn.

"Much obliged. My name's Napier," the man said, relaxing, resting his eyes. "Henk Willem Adriannus Van der Napier."

"Fancy that," Ki said. "It must tax your strength just to pack that handle around. What happened? Who shot you?"

But Napier had lapsed into unconsciousness again.

Shortly the proprietor returned with a steaming pitcher, an enamel basin, a bar of lye soap, soft cloths, a bottle of witch hazel and a tin of salve. Jessie untied the old makeshift bandages and now, with better light and hot soapy water, was able to cleanse Napier's head wound thoroughly. Her fingers were deft and tender as she worked, applying witch hazel and some salve, then wrapping his head in the fresh cloths. Finished, she stepped back, worried.

"It must really have hammered Napier when the slug hit. I'm afraid he should have a doctor look at

12

him, Ki, give him proper care. C'mon, we were headed for Beyond anyway. We can send the doctor back from there."

Leaving Napier tucked under the covers, they left the room and returned downstairs to the entrance with the proprietor. To him Jessie gave another dollar, saying, "This ought to cover the cost of Napier's room and corralling his horse. Do what you can for him. We'll have the doctor come out here as soon as possible."

The proprietor bit the coin, and pocketed it with a noncommittal grunt.

As the heavy door closed behind them, and they were heading for their mounts, Jessie remarked to Ki, "If Napier's horse is going to be tended to, I suspect we'd better do it ourselves."

All three horses were faring well, rested and watered, nibbling the weedy grass that fringed the trough. Ki untied the roan, and they began walking it over to the pole-fenced corral, which was off to one side, toward the rear of the inn. There were the dark shapes of three or four horses dozing within the enclosure. Otherwise all was still, no sight or sound of man or beast.

Or so it seemed—until Ki happened to glance across at the inn. They were almost to the corral, at a point where both the side and the rear of the inn were visible, and Ki's eye was caught by lamplight in one of the second floor windows. His first thought was that it came from Napier's room, which was curious, considering that Jessie had extinguished the lamp before they left. Then he realized the glow was from the room next door. Suddenly a figure moved to the window, illuminated by the lamp, and he saw the woman.

Tall, slender, with corn-silk blond hair cascading around her shoulders, for an instant the woman pressed her face against the windowpane, her expression frantic with fear. Just for an instant, and then the lamp was snuffed out and she disappeared into blackness.

It seemed to Ki in that split second of light that she beckoned urgently to him, yet he couldn't be sure. "Jessie?" he exclaimed, pointing. "Jessie, did you see the woman up there in that window?"

From the other side of the horse, Jessie sighed the sigh of an exasperated female. "I certainly did not. And if you had a speck of decency, you wouldn't be ogling innocent ladies who've forgotten to lower their blinds."

"She's in trouble—"

"And needs you to save her? I can just imagine how you'd like to. Really, Ki, we don't have time now for your shenanigans."

"Five minutes. Wait here, keep your eyes peeled, and if I'm not out in five minutes, come after me."

Ki ran back to the front entrance and tried the door, but it was bolted closed. He tested the window near the door, and when its sash refused to budge, he sprinted on around the building for another entry, and spotted an outside stairway leading to a fire-escape door in the gable of the inn. Ki clambered up the rickety steps to the landing and found the fire-escape door locked as well. But the upper half

14

of the door was of glass, painted a dingy brown to match the rest of the gable. The whole pane caved in before one jabbing punch of Ki's elbow. Brushing the glass remnants out of the doorway, Ki straddled his way inside, feet crunching on splintered window-pane. Ahead stretched the unlit corridor, a murky gray tunnel of doorways.

Ki fumbled along, trying to calculate which of the doors was to the room next to Napier's, the room where he'd seen the terrified woman. He was almost to that door when there was swift movement in the darkness. Someone careened against him. Ki pivoted, his own shadow a blot on the man's face, but he glimpsed a blur of gunmetal as the man swung the revolver he was gripping. Ki ducked, too late to evade the impact, the gun barrel clouting him on the side of the head. Lurching, gasping from pain, Ki charged in, slashing his left hand in a chop at the attacker's neck.

The attacker brought up a knee to Ki's groin, then they were both spilling to the hallway floor, rolling over and over. Ki had a momentary impression of the man's frenzied haste to escape from the scene, then the gun barrel thudded against his temple again and the man wrenched free, leaving a coat button in Ki's hand. Scrambling to his feet, the man aimed point-blank at Ki. Ki lunged up and forward, his shoulders hitting the man in the gut with a force that carried the man off his feet. The revolver discharged, shooting wild, then clattered against the wall and fell to the floor.

There was no time to grope for the fallen gun.

15

Gaining his footing, Ki saw steel flash as the attacker drew a knife out of a belt sheath. He deflected the stabbing thrust with his left forearm and drove a stiff-fingered right hand into the man. But stunned by the gun blast in his face, and staggered from the two blows to his head, Ki landed his punch slightly off-kilter, cracking a rib low on the man's chest. A harsh grunt of pain gusted from the man, the first sound he had uttered in the brief seconds of their brawling progress along the corridor.

Ki heard the scrape of boots as, hastily stumbling back to avoid his onslaught, the attacker turned and fled down the corridor. Ki took one step in pursuit, then he tripped on the revolver, which went skittering out from underfoot, and he found himself falling headlong. Before he could recover his balance, he heard a wild threshing in the corridor. The stairs echoed to a pounding clatter; somewhere in the building a gun thundered again.

Just then Jessie climbed through the broken window of the fire-escape door. "Hell's to pay!" she exclaimed, hurrying to Ki.

Ki, thrusting the coat button into his vest pocket, demanded, "Did you see anyone hotfooting out?"

"No, but I came running soon's I heard the shot."

"Might still catch 'em inside, then." Motioning for Jessie to follow, Ki tore down the corridor to the stairs and was descending to the tavern when he heard the unlatching of a door below. "Shit!"

Reaching the bottom of the stairs, they caught sight of a rear door swinging ajar at the end of the bar counter. On the floor nearby, the proprietor

16

sprawled lifeless in a pool of blood. And that, Ki reckoned, accounted for the shot he'd heard after his attacker had fled.

They raced for the door, sidestepping the body, just as a sudden noise of whinnying and galloping erupted outside. At the threshold they stopped, realizing it was useless to give further chase. Napier's roan and the other horses in the corral had been stampeded to cover the escape, and all Jessie and Ki could do was stand by and watch them scatter, listen to their hoofbeats diminish into the darkness.

"Well, leastwise I managed to snag this off the man's jacket," Ki growled, handing Jessie the button.

"Man? I thought you said you saw a woman."

"The woman!" Plunging back inside, Ki rushed upstairs to the door he'd never reached. That door was now wide open. Moving cautiously, he sparked a match alight, but the room was empty. Before the match burned out, he lit the wick of the still-warm lantern and went with Jessie over to the window from which the woman's face had been peering.

"Look here," Jessie gasped, "on the sill."

In the deep dust along the windowsill, a message had been traced by a finger. It read, "LAVERNA—TRIAD—HELP!"

"Triad . . . ," Ki mulled aloud. "The Triad Ranch, Winthrop Folgeron's spread. And the woman I saw here must be named Laverna. She needed help, okay. Somebody dragged her out, apparently, and I was in his way when he did it. Almost killed me, and he shot the proprietor dead to clear his path. You're

17

right, Jessie, there's hell to pay."

"Maybe the ruckus aroused Napier," Jessie suggested. "We ought to check on him, anyway. But who knows, he might've heard enough to be able to tell us something of what went on."

They headed directly from the girl's room to the room next door, wasting no time on ceremony. But the mysteriously wounded Henk Willem Adriannus Van der Napier had vanished into thin air.

★

Chapter 3

Morning came, and the Devil's Playground appeared with it, multicolored, far-lying, graven in startling clarity. It was still gray morning when Jessie and Ki reached Beyond, a small settlement, somnolent in the early hours and looking exactly what it was: ninety-three percent cattle, seven percent predators, badmen and short-card players.

The main drag of Beyond seemed to have been laid out haphazardly. Whoever had planned it undoubtedly never heard of the old saying about the closest distance between two points. Lined by false-fronted buildings with sagging wood awnings, slack-hipped stoops and tilted railings, the street wound and curved and, smack in the middle of town, made an abrupt, ninety-degree bend. There, in a square of dead grass, stood the only hotel, grandly misnamed the Ritz. At the far end of town, the weathered clapboards of a livery stable bulked like a huge misshapen box.

As Jessie and Ki rode into the yard of the livery, they were greeted by a white-headed oldster, who came out of the stable wiping his gnarled hands on a leather apron. "Help you?" the old hostler asked around a thick cud of blackstrap.

"Bed and feed for our horses," Jessie answered, dismounting.

"O'ernight?"

"Maybe longer."

"Includin' rubdown, that'll be seventy-five cents per critter tonight, sixty cents each day after."

"Mite high."

"Depends how you look at it." The old man spat a thin stream of juice into the dirt and squinted challengingly.

Jessie shrugged, too tired to argue. Indeed, both she and Ki were more exhausted than hungry, from riding day and night, and would breakfast later. Likewise, Jessie planned to seek out the law and report the death at Halfway Inn.

Toting their traveling bags—Jessie had a small bellows case, and Ki carried a gladstone—they walked back down the street to the Ritz. Compared to its neighbors, the hotel was a nice enough looking place, two-storied like the Halfway Inn, but with a gallery running along the front. It had been painted, too, one coat probably, on wood so thirsty that it looked dyed instead of painted, a faint powdery blue. Inside, the lobby had the distinct air of a faded parlor. The prissily dressed, gimlet-eyed young clerk at the reception desk had a different air about him, that of *eau de lilac*.

Approaching the desk, Jessie glanced at a fly-specked calendar pinned to the wall in back of the

20

clerk and asked, "This is the twenty-first, isn't it?"

"Yes'm, all day today," the clerk replied, reversing the room register for her to sign.

The register was a big leather and mahogany book on a swivel with a silver-plated bell above it, as one might expect in San Francisco. The previous person signing in had scrawled "Stonewall Jackson, Washington, D.C., stall number seven," showing how seriously some guests took the register. But Jessie wrote her name correctly in plain, bold print, and so did Ki, for she had advised Folgeron that they would arrive on or about the twenty-first, and they didn't want to chance a missed connection.

"Adjoining rooms, twelve and fourteen." Without looking, the clerk grabbed a couple of keys from the rack behind him. "Second floor, at the end of the passage."

The upstairs corridor was lighted by beef-tallow dips in nickled reflectors, one of which hung opposite a door with the number "12" put on it with paint that looked like tar. Entering, Jessie found the room to be in keeping with the rest of the hotel, with an iron cot, a washstand and blue china bowl and pitcher, and an old carved-oak wardrobe. On the side of the room opposite the cot, a dreary red curtain hung from a rail, covering, she assumed, a communicating door to Ki's room.

Locking the door, Jessie sat on the edge of the cot and, sighing, pulled off her boots. The floor was cold to her feet as she padded across to draw the window drapes, then back to get a fresh change of clothes out of her bellows bag. She then stripped naked, filled the basin with water from the pitcher, and used a hand towel to scrub herself. As much as she would have loved a hot bath, that luxury was not possible at the tubless Ritz. Constantly rinsing out the towel, she made do by sluicing off a good portion of the Devil's Playground that was dusting her skin. Briskly she dried herself and dressed in clean clothing, then pinned up her hair and climbed into bed. She was asleep almost the instant her head hit the pillow.

She was awakened by a stranger.

She felt his presence at first, and opening her eyes, she saw him. He was hovering over her open bag, not pawing through it, but giving its contents an interested scrutiny. Hearing Jessie stir, he straightened and turned, his button eyes boring into her in a swift, appraising look.

"Well, now, what have we here?" he said, more or less to himself.

"A burglar, that's what," Jessie retorted, in no mood to tolerate the way the man was eyeing her as she sat up. Her holstered pistol was hanging by its shell belt from the back of the chair, but she had learned from experience to sleep with her derringer handy and now drew it from under the pillow, pointing it at him. "Get out, and I'll call the matter closed, if not forgotten."

"Whoa there, Miz Starbuck, let's not be hasty," the man said, abruptly losing his smugness. "I'm Winthrop Folgeron. Y'see? Here's my headband to identify me by."

A lanky man, Folgeron had a high forehead deeply creased by wrinkles, topped by sparse graying hair

22

neatly plastered to the skull. Just above the ears, about hatbrim height, he was wearing a wide headband of threaded stone beads and intricately braided leather of some kind. It appeared to be very worn, very old, and he handled it carefully as he removed it to show Jessie.

"Made of mountain goat," he explained. "A unique ceremonial artifact of the Tukudeka, or Sheepeaters, tribe. They're regarded as renegade Bannocks and Shoshoni, isolated and nomadic in their sacred mountains, feared for their savagery and a poison for arrows they extract from some root. The band is part of my collection, and seems to help keep my crew in line. Many of 'em are breeds, a superstitious lot," he added confidentially, slipping the headband back on. "But please, pardon my method of entrance. Beyond is a town of enemies."

"Enemies? Surely not due to your photography."

"No, m'dear. The consequence of wealth and a collector's zeal. I retired to a big ranch overlapping three borders—Nevada, Oregon and Idaho— and have since expanded my holdings as opportunities arose. My business advisor and attorney, Mr. Enoch Hyde of San Francisco, is well versed in discovering loopholes in haphazard land grants. Alas, some of the ranchers I dispossessed are bitter. They've ganged up against me, calling themselves the Revengers, and've vowed to kill me on sight."

"Then you'd best not stay here any longer than you have to, Mr. Folgeron. What's the matter of national importance you're so eager to see me about?"

Folgeron pursed his lips, as though pondering his

answer judiciously, and gripped the collar lapels of his loose, brown duck jacket. He looked like a prosperous stockman. Almost. Somehow, though, he was a bit too immaculate for a working stockman. A stockman would have had at least one stain on that jacket, and baggy pockets filled with just about everything.

"International, actually," he began after a moment. "On one of my last photographic expeditions for the Department of the Interior, I heard native rumorings about a tomb. A royal tomb containing the body of an ancient Mayan king, lying hidden in the depths of a massive stone temple near Palenque, at Chiapas, Mexico. Think of it! Well, after much research, I've concluded the tomb exists, and have pinpointed where the temple should be located."

"That would be a stupendous find, true enough, but I fail to see how it concerns me."

"The temple is in an area controlled by the Yucatan Mine and Development Company. Yucatan is a subsidiary of Veterano S.A., which in turn is operated by Fundador Industries, a branch of Allied, a Starbuck holding corporation."

"In other words—"

"In other words, m'dear, you own that area."

"I'm impressed. You've done your homework fairly well, except that I'm sure Yucatan only leases the land. Besides, getting permission from Yucatan or Starbuck to go hunt for the tomb would be just a formality. You need to arrange it through the Mexican government, the Director of the Office of Prehistoric Monuments."

"Mexican meddling?" Folgeron looked aghast. "No, no, the temple's treasures must be recovered privately, removed by your companies to the United States. To the Smithsonian, perhaps, or the Museum of Natural History. It's our duty to preserve them for posterity."

"Not to mention steal their glory."

"Harsh words." Now he tried to look humble, but couldn't quite make it. "But think, m'dear! Think of the sarcophagus, the mosaic death mask, the pearl and jade religious accoutrements . . . Why, we'll have the the archaeological dig of the century, rivaling Egyptian antiquities."

"I am thinking, Mr. Folgeron. I'm thinking your proposition will require a great deal of thinking over."

"Unfortunately, there's no time to spare, particularily after this winter's delay. We must go begin preparations at Palenque at once."

"Very well, let's meet at your ranch this evening, and I'll give you my decision then."

"Under normal circumstances, I'd be honored to have you as my guest. But right now the Triad is an armed enclave against the Revengers, with six-strand barbed wire fencing and padlocked gates, and guards patrolling round the clock. To avoid your risking a mishap, I'd druther endanger myself and contact you here tonight." With a martyred expression, Folgeron then produced a wallet. "Naturally, all that's transpired is to be kept secret between us. How much do I owe you for the trouble of coming here?"

"Nary a cent," Jessie replied, and indicated the door. "Good-bye for now, Mr. Folgeron. Rest assured our business will remain confidential."

Folgeron cracked open the door, peered both ways, then hastened out and down the empty corridor. As soon as he was gone, Jessie examined the door lock and jamb plate, finding they hadn't been forced. She wasn't much surprised. Closing the door, she was wondering whether it would be worth getting the key and relocking it, when Ki moved out from behind the curtain covering the connecting doorway, wearing only his jeans, his bare feet noiseless on the floor.

Jessie smiled. "Don't you know it's impolite to eavesdrop?"

"Next time you entertain gentlemen, post a 'do not disturb' sign," Ki retorted. Then he added with a snort, "Some gent. What do you think of his crazy scheme?"

"Crazier ones than his have proven true. But in any case, I want no part of it."

"That's your final answer?"

"Final. It's not only unethical, it'd jeopardize our license to operate in Mexico."

"Then why didn't you tell him no? Why'd you lead him on?"

"Because I wanted to wangle an invite to his place. Now, put on a shirt, and let's get breakfast. We've got some riding to do. I still aim to see the inside of Triad Ranch."

"What for?"

"Have you forgotten Laverna, the lady who left a

message for help?" Jessie delved into her pocket and brought out the button Ki had torn from the coat of the attacker at Halfway Inn. "This matches the buttons on the coat worn by my late visitor, Winthrop Folgeron. And one of his is missing."

"It doesn't make sense. Why would Folgeron have snatched Laverna? Why any of this?" Ki demanded. "All there's been so far is question marks. Jessie, I've a hunch we're up against devils aplenty in Devil's Playground."

"It sounds like it," she agreed, for there was the heavy tramp of many boots out in the corridor.

The china doorknob turned and a half-dozen men barged into the room, with another handful crowding through the connecting door behind Ki. They were wearing common range garb, faded and frayed, and had the haggard countenances typical of small independent ranchers struggling to make ends meet. At the moment they appeared strained and wrung out, their voices chorusing in a growling rumble, one lifting louder than the rest.

"Now where did Folgeron light off to?"

Jessie shrugged. "I think," she remarked to Ki, "that we've just run into the Revengers."

"You ain't just salivatin', gal," the loudmouthed man responded. He was ponderous, barrel-waisted and bull-necked, with a shock of wild red hair and a wide mattress of beard spreading down his brawny chest. The loose skin around his mouth was sucked in, as though he were getting set to spout something more, when another man rushed in and thrust the hotel register at him.

"Looky, Otis, they's from Texas."

The redhead called Otis glanced at the register, then at Jessie and Ki. "And who can prove different?" he said, with offensive jollity. "And what brung y'all so far from home, I reckon, was to meet up with Folgeron. Tell me if'n I'm right."

Jessie said, "No, you tell me what y'all are doing, bustin' in here, and I'll tell you if that's right or not."

Otis, steaming under Jessie's rebuff, trying to hide it, said, "One of the boys here saw Folgeron scalawaggin' away from the hotel. He wasn't close enough to snap off a shot, but there wasn't no mistakin' that Injun headband. When he told us about it, we come here and checked to see who Folgeron might've been visitin'. There was only two strangers registered— you two! Now, what were you and that varmint palaverin' about?"

"It was personal business," Jessie replied civilly, "and none of yours."

One of the men hooted, "We done caught us a spitfire."

"P'raps she'll sweeten if we jug her awhile," another man snapped. "Same for her silent pard, here. P'raps he'll find a tongue."

Ki, who prided himself on keeping cool and collected in the face of adversity, began losing patience. "Miss Starbuck told you, what she and Folgeron talked about didn't have a blasted thing to do with you folks. So step aside. We're hungry and're going to go get something to eat."

He felt a gun muzzle in the small of his back. From

behind him, a bleary eyed small-time rancher said, "Not till Mist' Muell is done with you."

"And that might be some time." Otis grinned, and seeming satisfied that they were unarmed, what with Ki wearing only pants and Jessie's pistol hanging on the chair, he said pompously, "Okay, boys, escort 'em to that empty storeroom behind Grover's. We can question 'em there later, undisturbed."

"Not so fast," Ki said. "I'm not ready to go anywhere on your say-so." His voice was ice cold. "Who is the law here?"

"He is," said the man covering Ki. "You're looking at him in person. Mr. Otis Muell."

"I never heard of no law named Mister," Ki said. "They're generally Sheriff or Deputy or Marshal."

"There's none of that other kind of law, the kind you're referrin' to, closer'n Twin Falls. He wasn't elected. He was chose."

"Who chose him?" Ki asked. "You and your friends here and him, in the dark o' night, in a privy somewhere?"

"Simmer down," Jessie said soothingly.

"He was chose," the man replied, "by the parties you named, but not in a place like you named, plus the entire community of Beyond to officiate for us in that capacity." He prodded Ki in the ribs. "You heard Mist' Muell."

"You heard him," said the man with the hotel register. "Move!"

Jessie started for the door. Ki stood frozen.

Otis Muell stepped over, shoved his face into Ki's and bawled, "That's an order!"

"I never seemed somehow to take orders too good," Ki said in a low voice.

And now a firm grasp was around Ki's biceps, Jessie's. "Oh, yes, he does," she said. "He loves orders."

Reluctantly, Ki allowed Jessie to lead him to the door.

Chapter 4

Grouping in around, covering them with their guns, the Revengers herded Jessie and Ki along the hall and downstairs through the lobby. On their way outside, the man with the register dumped it back on the desk. The clerk was nowhere to be seen, which was a smart play on his part, Jessie reckoned.

They moved on down the street. It was late in the morning now, elevenish to judge by the sun, and locals were out and about. Every pair of eyes they passed, taking in the procession, glared. Nobody was partial to strangers, any strangers, today.

Near the outskirts of town, behind a row of buildings, Otis Muell gestured Jessie and Ki through a door. They found themselves in a big empty room, dust-moted from a cracked, barred window in the outer wall. It was cold, dim, and from the smell of it, Jessie decided it had once been used as a grain and feed storeroom.

"Set," Muell said, and pointed down.

Ki sat cross-legged on the bare floor. Jessie pulled up an empty box and perched herself on the edge of it, about ten feet from her captors.

"Ain't et yet, eh? I'll have your lunches and suppers sent over to you from the café," Muell said. "Out of our own pocket, I might add."

"Lunches and suppers?" Jessie said. "Hold us how long?"

"Up to you," Muell said. "When you feel like talking, holler." He walked away with his friends, the other Revengers, and the door was swung shut and padlocked.

Instantly Ki was at the window, testing the bars, but they were firmly embedded in a wooden frame. "Relax," Jessie advised, preparing to do just that. She had her derringer secreted behind her buckle, in case worse came to worst; but to have drawn it up in the room could've sparked a general massacre, and down here she'd have to get someone alone and close enough for it to do much good. Anyway, her impression was that the Revengers were more mistaken than downright mean. And besides, she was curious to see what might develop. Some answers, hopefully.

Presently another one of the Revengers returned, edging into the room with two bowls of soup on a tray, a revolver held in his free hand and a couple of slices of wadded-up bread in the clinch of his armpit. Serving the food, he sat down opposite them, leaning against the door. "Chow down. 'Course, you make some kind of move I took the wrong way, and I got excited and cut loose on you, it wouldn't be personal. You understand?"

"I'm afraid I do," Jessie said, and studied the soup for a moment. "What kind is it?"

"Vegetable."

"Wonderful," Ki muttered, as they began to eat. The man's fixed gaze returned their glances. They saw watery, red-rimmed, dull eyes, a harsh self-pitying mouth and enough encrusted grime on a crinkled neck to raise a crop of potatoes. There was a nasty vagueness about this fellow that Ki didn't much care for. Nevertheless, Ki sounded him out.

"Are you a rancher hereabouts?" he asked conversationally.

"I was, afore Folgeron ousted me. Truth tell, my spread was failing. The only thing that ever come into my life that didn't whipsaw me was that trolley I run back in Cincinnati."

"Then why don't you go back to Cincinnati?"

"And leave all this golden opportunity out here? No, sirree! For one thing it cost me too much to get here. It cost me a sixteen-year-old bride, six pigs, two cows and a team of blue mules."

"So you're going to stick it out?"

"Of course. There's fortunes to be made here, if you know cows."

"Do you know cows?"

"Not too well. They seem to know me better'n I know them."

Jessie, listening to all this, dished up a spoonful of soup and found a little bone button in it, the kind one might find on a nightshirt. "What's this?" she asked.

"You're eating vegetable soup," the man said. "Many a this and that goes into vegetable soup."

Jessie studied it a moment. "Is it eatable?"

33

"Mildred o'er the café throwed some leftover hash in the soup," the man answered. "It was in the hash. If it was eatable in the hash, then it's eatable in the soup. That's logic, ain't it?"

Jessie laid the button on the tray. "Saving it for later," she explained.

She and Ki ate the soup, however, and the bread, and felt better.

"We ain't meaning to be too harsh," the man said, stacking the soup bowls and picking up the tray. "If you've bucked Triad Ranch the way we've bucked it, you'd be on the prod, too. Want me to fetch Mist' Muell?"

"Nothing I can tell him I didn't before," Jessie said. "Folgeron wanted to discuss a deal that has no connection with your troubles. Sorry."

The man scowled. "Sorry y'self. We can't take chances. If we let you loose, it might mean that pretty soon you'll be in cahoots with Folgeron. Someday we're going to find our way through that fence. We'll have enough guns against us when that happens. Them crew of Folgeron's can shoot, specially his blood-crazy *segundo,* Blackjack Queeg, who ramrods the outfit. As long as you're locked in here, that makes two less against us."

Once again the door was shut and bolted.

Restless, Ki went and peered out the barred window. "We're getting no place so fast, we'll likely meet ourselves coming back."

Jessie couldn't think of anything to add to that.

It was while Ki was still gazing from the window that he suddenly beckoned Jessie over. "Do I see it?"

34

he demanded. "Or am I loco?"

For, emerging from the rocky undergrowth off back of the building, the elusive Henk Willem Adriannus Van der Napier came strolling toward the window, chomping an apple.

"I heard they had you cached here," he said genially, drawing close to the bars. "What've you got yourselves into?"

"Hard to say," Jessie admitted. "I'm not too sure myself."

"Well, here I am, beholdin' for last night, to get you out." Finishing his apple, Napier inspected the window, his face still unshaven and forehead still bandaged, although since last seen he'd aquired a mangy slouch hat. He sort of resembled a pirate, Jessie thought, but not so tough that women mightn't be tempted to look at him a bit wistfully. From a belt sheath, then, he took a long-bladed hunting knife and laid it between the bars. "The wood should chip away with a li'le whittling, I reckon."

"Thanks, Mr. Napier, only—"

"Dutch. Call me Dutch, if I may call you Jessie." Flashing a grin, he began striding back toward the rocks and underbrush.

"Wait a minute!" Jessie shouted after him. "I've got a lot to ask you!"

But Dutch Napier had already disappeared.

Jessie and Ki fell to work with the knife at once, chipping away at the wooded base in which the bars were imbedded. It was slow, arduous labor, but at last they had two of the bars freed from the base. Ki put his strength against the iron and was able to wrench these bars outward. Jessie squeezed through the opening, Ki following.

"Free!" Jessie gasped triumphantly, leaning against the shed.

"Free, half-naked and weaponless," Ki noted. "What say we get our stuff, get our horses, and get going while the gettin's good."

Racing along the rear of the buildings, keeping to cover as much as possible, they headed back to the Ritz. There was a rear door to the hotel, and finding it unlocked, they eased inside, hardly daring to breathe again until they'd reached the dubious shelter of the lobby. Blessedly, it was deserted save for the young clerk, whose eyes rolled wide in utter astonishment when they entered.

"Watch him close, Jessie," Ki said with a menacing scowl. "There ain't supposed to be no killin', but make an exception if he raises the slightest squawk. I'll be right back."

The clerk gave a strangled peep, trembling as he watched Ki hurry up the stairs to the rooms they'd rented that morning.

Jessie added her own intimidation, stabbing Napier's knife into the desk counter. "I don't appreciate you letting Folgeron into my room."

"I-I never! He must've s-snuck by me, the back way, 'cause I never even knowed he was here till the Revengers come burstin' in after him. Honest!"

"Uh-huh. I had my door locked."

"Pshaw, Miz S-Starbuck, that don't matter. Any key fits any lock."

Bounding downstairs, Ki returned fully dressed, hauling his gladstone and Jessie's bag, boots, denim jacket and shell belt. Swiftly Jessie donned her jacket and boots and strapped on her pistol, then turned, starting for the rear entrance with Ki.

"Hold on!" the clerk called in a quavering voice.

He was probing deep under the desk, and Jessie spun about, raising her gun, fearful that the clerk was going for a hidden weapon. But his hands had come into view again, and in them was a wax-sealed envelope.

"What's this?" Jessie asked suspiciously.

"Look," the clerk said, "it ain't healthy to side against the Revengers. But Mist' Folgeron paid me to do a job, and I don't want him mad at me, neither. Y'see, a couple of weeks ago he visited me private-like, and told me you'd be arriving in Beyond about the twenty-first, and to give you this letter personal."

Jessie took the envelope and ran her thumb under the flap, breaking the wax seal. The note that was enclosed was written in Folgeron's unmistakable, broad scrawl.

Dear Miss Starbuck:

Perhaps I'll be unable to meet you in Beyond as originally planned. Perhaps not. I've reason to fear for my life. If we do manage to meet, I'll inform you fully of the situation. If not, you'll find an explanatory document hidden in my library at Triad Ranch. Look for *Magistrate System of Attica, 330 B.C.*, the third book from the left on the fourth shelf from the floor nearest the big door. Good luck, and take care.

Y'r m'st ob'd'nt s'rv'nt,
Winthrop Folgeron

Wordlessly Jessie handed the note to Ki, then faced the clerk, laying a dollar on the desk. "Keep your mouth shut about this and you won't get into any trouble. Now tell me—what did Winthrop Folgeron look like?"

"No different than usual. Big, bearded, bald as ever, wearing that wretched headband of his and—"

A salvo of gunshots erupted outside somewhere.

Jessie could well guess where, and Ki seconded her notion. "Somebody's discovered we've flown the coop!" They dashed for the rear exit, bags in hand, leaving the desk clerk agape.

Outside, they took a quick glance down the street. Advancing from the direction of the shed, the gang of Revengers was swelling into a mob, gathering steam and support from boardwalk loafers and mischief-makers.

"Them goddamn strangers escaped!"

"Where?"

"Away, you idiot! C'mon, we gotta hunt 'em down!"

In a slight crouch Jessie and Ki sprinted across the hotel grounds and on up behind the line of buildings, toward the livery stable. Reaching the rear of the livery without detection, they darted alongside the stable barn to the front and spotted the old hostler standing out in the yard. They hunkered for a moment, gauging their chances—which appeared slim to none, until the hostler started a few steps down the street, shaking his fist in agreement with the oncoming Revengers.

Jessie and Ki softly toed around toward the open stable doors, glimpsing the crowd encroaching on the hotel now, some of the more courageous fanning out to search the vicinity. They dipped inside the barn. Quickly yet as quietly as they could, they located their mounts and led them out of the stalls to saddle. They hoped to hide whatever noise they were making in the clamor of the hunt, and in the skittish way the other horses were prancing and nickering in their stalls, as if spooked by the feral scent of the death-wish mob.

Then closer, much closer, they heard, "Who's there?"

They swiveled and crouched against the splintered wheel of a rotting freight wagon, motionless in the dimness as the hostler entered the barn in a sort of gnarled trot. Spying the pinto and sorrel, he grumbled and spat and moved disgustedly toward them.

"How'd you get out? Hey, and how'd your saddles—"

The hostler ended his question in a choke. Ki, rising behind him as he passed, clamped a hand over the hostler's mouth. The hostler made gargling noises and tried clawing at the hand.

"Stop it!" Jessie snapped. "We don't want to hurt you."

The hostler's struggles subsided, though his eyes

glared as if on fire. "All we're after is our horses," Jessie assured him. "Now are you going to be quiet?" The hostler nodded, and Ki removed his hand.

"Help!" the hostler instantly yelled. "It's them strangers!"

This time Ki interrupted him with a chopping fist to the jaw. The hostler's teeth clacked together and his head snapped back, whipping his body off his feet. He dropped flat on his back atop a pile of manured hay, stunned but still obstinately trying to shout.

"Help!" It came out garbled, but effective. "It's them!"

Boots came pounding, a lot of them. Swearing, unladylike, Jessie vaulted into the saddle. Ki grabbed for the reins, but his boogered sorrel shied away, and his foot missed the stirrups the first couple of tries. "You damn old coot, you! I just bet you'd love for us to get caught, just so's you can claim our horses!"

"Them jiggers is gettin' away!" Up the street spewed the mob, firing wildly as they ran. "Shoot 'em! Shoot 'em down!"

A bullet kicked splinters from the wall alongside Jessie as she and Ki launched charging out of the barn. Their horses, already fractious, tore off in a mad gallop in the wrong direction, down the street straight for the mob—who stopped, wavering uncertainly. Holding on for dear life, Jessie fired her pistol over their heads. Windows shattered. The mob broke. The courageous men scrambled for the boardwalks, overturning benches and tripping over hitching rails; and a few, on hands and knees, scuttled under the bat wings of the nearest saloon.

Jessie and Ki kept low over their flying horses, urging them on. By the time the mob was able to collect its addled wits again, they were past the last of Beyond's buildings and hitting the trail on which they'd entered town. At the first fork they came to, they cut off onto a branch trail that paralleled a deep dry wash, while behind them in Beyond raged utter confusion, the Revengers scrambling for horses to give chase.

Jessie and Ki's mounts were feisty and kept straining to run. So Jessie and Ki let them, gratified by the way they settled into a stretching cadence northward. The branch angled away from the dry wash and up the long grade of a hillock. From its crest, they could glimpse bobbing figures not all that far behind, dogging their dust-plumed trail. They could hear the distant shouts, the occasional gunshot, and they chided themselves. They had no plans, no place to hide, nothing. Nothing except an infuriated mob on their tail, veritably foaming at the mouth for revenge.

As an escape, this one left quite a bit to be desired.

★

Chapter 5

Raking the flanks of their horses, Jessie and Ki plunged down the other side of the hillock. At the bottom, they veered off the trail and charged pell-mell through the dark masses of boulders and scrub toward the dry-wash bed. The bed at this point ran narrow and deep, like an arroyo, and they had trouble controlling their mounts as they skidded down one bank and clambered up the other. They wheeled and crossed again, then recrossed a third and a fourth time. The packed, eroded dirt and gravelly sand cratered around their tracks, filling and flattening the depressions, so that all sense of direction was confused.

They started back toward the trail on the same path they'd made getting to the dry-wash bed. When they spied the Revengers' posse cresting the hillock, they slowed to a dustless walk and, under cover of boulders and scrub thickets, cautiously began moving southerly, as if to return to Beyond.

The Revengers hit bottom and almost passed where Jessie and Ki had left the trail before someone spotted their path. They reined in. So did Jessie and Ki, hiding motionless a short distance away in a thatch of twisted sagebrush, hands over their streaming horses' mouths to stifle any whinnies. The posse milled, then roared off toward the dry-wash bed.

Immediately Jessie and Ki angled back to their path, their own prints becoming lost in the welter of the posse tracks. Then, instead of heading back on the main trail to Beyond, they detoured around the town and continued on south. Twilight fell softly and quietly as they twisted through eroded culverts and between massive boulders, forging a route designed to conceal them from view. The terrain gradually rose to become foothills, and they began climbing through a series of connecting valleys and canyons, turning westerly now with the spine of the hills. Night enveloped them by the time they reined in by a small rill which cut down through a craggy ledge, and they dismounted, stiff and exhausted.

Their trembling, heaving mounts sunk muzzles gratefully to the water and nearby scratchgrass. They, too, drank from the stream, though for them there was nothing they could do for food, except pull up their belts a notch. The pale moon, merging from behind banked clouds, illuminated the flats below—where somewhere, quite likely, rode the Revengers still rabid to catch them. Posses were known to pursue someone for as much as a hundred miles, holding court where they caught him, and dispatching him as summarily as possible.

"And sooner or later," Ki observed, "they'll realize we're not ahead of them, and then they'll start looking for tracks."

Slewing down out of the hills, they continued straight—or as straight as the land would allow—across heat-seared plateaus, through mesa-flanking bench and brush-strewn cutbanks. Shortly, after passing through a straggly belt of tamarack, they came upon a path, thread-thin and rarely used, that wriggled in the same direction. Veering, they followed the path as it skirted some jagged sandstone rises, doglegged around the last one and intersected another trail, this one more along the lines of a ranch-wagon road.

They took the road. It was risky, but their horses were simply too exhausted to continue forging overland. The wagon road was also bearing west, although like most such trails, it took the roundabout, easy way, leading, in turn, to each ranch en route. From what little Jessie and Ki could make out in passing, the landscape consisted of meager rangeland and occasional acreages, of hardy grasses and prickly thickets and clumps of bedded livestock, and rocks—endless stretches of rocks, lost in the dark indigo of night.

Presently the wagon road encountered a stock fence and began running alongside its stout, six-strand barbed wire length. Jessie, studying the fence speculatively, remarked, "Ki, this's the kind of fence Folgeron described. We must be bordering Triad Ranch."

"Makes sense, Jessie. If I've got this country figured out right, we've cut onto the main trail from Beyond, the one heading out of town past the livery. Do you want to keep on going thisaway and call on Winthrop Folgeron?"

"More than ever." Jessie frowned thoughtfully. "Do you recall how the hotel clerk described Folgeron? Big, bearded and bald. It certainly doesn't fit the man who visited me this morning with that Mexican proposition. He must've been an imposter, wearing Folgeron's headband. Just what his game was, I don't know. But the real Winthrop Folgeron asked us here for something important—and dangerous—and we've got to get inside Triad Ranch, I bet, to find some answers and straighten out this mess."

After a bit they came upon a series of low knolls, like bunched knuckles, and the fence went around one side while the trail wound along the other flank. Verging on a blind curve, Jessie and Ki rode without speaking, concerned about their mounts' flagging energies. Suddenly, without warning, from the other side of the blind curve, a swarm of flickering shadows barged into view. The swarm resolved into mounted men, perhaps two dozen, and they were nearly over Jessie and Ki. They reined like maniacs.

The men were so close that at first it seemed all enormous horses' chests and heads and bridles, leather bridle straps and brass buckles, flying streamers of slaver. Then loomed the men behind the horses' ears, half-raised in their saddles. It was a toss-up who was more astonished—Jessie and Ki, or the riders. The difference was, the riders had the initiative. At the instant of their surprise, many were carrying their rifles, not in their rifle boots, but out and slantwise across the inside of their saddleforks, hair-trigger ready for a snap-shot.

These boys weren't on an after-dinner mosey, Jessie and Ki knew; they were out hunting blood and mayhem, rarin' to shoot on sight.

Jessie and Ki were startled, but not so much that they didn't react. Instinctively, Ki jabbed his sorrel into full gallop. Jessie was a heartbeat behind, reflexively spurring her pinto on, figuring, like Ki, that their best response was to somehow break through the crunch of riders and cut aside, into the knolls. But as they charged the pileup, a handful of men dived from horseback and tackled Jessie and Ki out of their saddles, bearing them to the ground.

The others, dismounting, clustered around as Jessie and Ki were hauled to a stand. Only one among them remained on horseback; he pressed forward and sat his saddle, looking down at the prisoners.

Catching her breath, Jessie ignored the man on horseback and stared at the others first. Ki, too, checked around so that he would know them again, whenever and wherever he might see them. Lean-bodied, hard-faced, they had all been cut from the same mold. They were dressed like rangehands and their clothes had seen much use, but unlike common cowpokes, they wore gun and knife in a manner that showed they were not ornaments. And there was a certain coyote tightness about them that tabbed them as renegades in from either the desert or some reservation.

The man on horseback demanded, "What brung you here?"

Woodenly, Jessie raised her gaze to the man. Wicked little eyes glared down at her from between slotted, membranous eyelids, and he chewed away rhythmically at nothing with a mouth that, from nostrils to either side of the jaw, was flat and bladderlike. Remembering the Revenger's reference to the *segundo* who ramrodded Winthrop Folgeron's crew, Jessie reckoned this must be the blood-crazy Blackjack Queeg. Like the others, he was clad in range garb and had a thong-tied holster and utilitarian shell belt. But judging from his aura of arrogance and domination, it simply couldn't be anyone else.

"I'm Jessica Starbuck and this is my companion, Ki," she answered. "Likely your boss has spoken to you about us."

She wasn't prepared for the fitful giggle that came, like spasms, from Blackjack Queeg. "This's luck," Queeg said, but he was addressing his crew. "Tie their hands behind 'em and drag 'em along. To the boneyard across the creek. It'll be a fittin' place to leave the pair of 'em."

"Wait!" Ki snapped. "Hold on!"

The Triad hands were of no mind to. "Grab 'em!" one bellowed, and they crowded in, leveling guns, a couple of them fetching coiled saddle ropes.

Jessie knew they were in for it. This misguided mob was comprised of Triad men, Folgeron hired hands and therefore Starbuck allies, yet she couldn't

47

very well stand idle and let them maim or possibly kill her and Ki. In desperation, she elbowed a gunman, kicked the shins of one of the men holding ropes, and sprang at Blackjack Queeg, grabbing him by the leg.

"Leggo! Leggo!" Queeg barked, trying to shake free.

But Jessie clung tightly and, with a wrenching yank, ripped Queeg loose of his saddle. Off he catapulted, getting a taste of his own medicine. Jessie gave him an extra dose as she pulled him down, planting a fist into the center of his startled face. There was a muffled crunch, and Queeg howled, sprawling flat in wild, flailing motions. Jessie stepped back—

And many hands piled in on her, clamping her arms. Jessie jerked and whipsawed, shaking off one armlock, only to be caught in another, crying out as muscles and tendons were twisted painfully. Still she struggled, but she was overwhelmed, unable to reach her weapons, unable to break the gang's hold.

Ki as well launched an attack. He lashed high with a leaping kick, tempering its normally fatal force, wishing only to incapacitate. He caught the nearest Triad crewman in the solar plexus, landed, and kicked again, his slipper this time scooping dirt and spraying it into the faces of the two other men. The first man was falling to his knees, clutching his belly; the second duo pawed grit out of their eyes and blindly swung their revolvers. The rest of the hands, those not grappling with Jessie, piled onto Ki, snagging his legs and arms and pistol-whipping him, driving him to the ground. He struggled to rise, both arms gripped tightly by men who hung on and tried to keep him down.

With Jessie subdued, more crewmen swarmed on Ki, clutching his legs and hanging on. He was kicked in the ribs; a boot heel stomped the small of his back and missed his spine by a fraction of an inch. Grimly enduring the pain, he battled upright to his knees, then to his feet. He shook off one and kidney-punched another in a wildness born of fury and frustration. Another yelp went up; another crewman went spinning aside and bowling into Blackjack Queeg, who was blearily recovering.

"Shoot him!" Queeg raged nasally, his nostrils spurting blood. "No, don't! You're too close! You'll shoot each other!"

Defiantly Ki resisted, managing to dish out some of the considerable savagery of which he was capable. Using elbow smashes, kicks, punches and open-handed strikes, he brought anguished wails to some and wheezing groans to others, sending them skidding, stumbling, falling to their hands and knees. But there were too many of them, and the odds took their toll. And the gun butts hammered, hammered, hammered at Ki's head with stunning force. Already suffering from the gun-clubbing fight last night, Ki felt himself sinking, almost blacking out.

Before he could recover, his arms were jerked behind his back and his wrists securely bound. Jessie's hands were likewise tied behind her with rope. Their bolted horses were recovered by Triad hands, and they were boosted to their own saddles.

Although they were not disarmed, their weapons seemed as far away as the cold moon above.

With Blackjack Queeg riding up front, the group started back the way they had come, the way Jessie and Ki had been heading when they'd all collided. Less than a mile downtrail, the knolls declined and the big fence came back into view, and pretty soon the trail was intersected by a private lane—a lane that cut off to the west and was blocked at the fence line by a wrought-iron, padlocked gate. This was most obviously the entrance to Folgeron's Triad Ranch.

Dismounting at the gate, Queeg probed at the padlock with a key. When the gate swung open, he remounted and gestured for his crew to follow, riding the lane up a shallow rise. About a hundred yards up the slope, on a shelf of level ground, stood an ancient cemetery. Gravesites were marked by headstones, although some graves had been dug and then left as vacant pits, perhaps to be filled at a later date with the empty, crude pineboard coffins that lay scattered about.

There Queeg called a halt, and while his crew was dismounting, he began riding back and forth as if he were on fancy parade. "Okay, boys, stand these trespassers alongside buryin' holes," he commanded in a flat-toned voice, a hand clamped over his mashed, bloody nose. "Six o' you form a firin' squad. Get your minds off whiskey and women long enough to hold a bead."

Roughly Jessie and Ki were hauled off their mounts and positioned beside two open graves. A half-dozen crewmen with saddle carbines lined up facing them, their expressions shrouded by darkness. But if Jessie couldn't tell what they thought of committing execution-style murder, she sure as hell knew how she felt about it. And she voiced her opinion, arguing strongly and somewhat profanely, ending with:

"Maybe it's custom at Triad Ranch to kill folks who come near the fence, Queeg, but it happens we were to meet with Folgeron tonight. Your boss's going to be mighty sore about this when he hears the news."

"I don't think Folgeron's gonna hear nothin'." Queeg gave another of his maniacal snickers. "Yes'm, so far as my boss is concerned, you're gonna be a dead issue."

Ki hadn't spoken since they'd been captured, figuring it was useless, and instead had concentrated on rebuilding his strength. Now, while standing beside the grave, he began freeing his wrists from the rope. Focusing on the task, he purposely dislocated the bones of his wrists, then his hands, even his nimble fingers, as swiftly yet secretly as possible, hoping he'd have enough time to get loose and fight back.

"Ready!" Queeg lifted his hat and stood in his stirrups as he rode out of the line of fire. The men of his firing squad shifted carbines they had cuddled in their left arms. Ki twisted and stretched his ligaments and muscles, gradually worming his limp, formless flesh through the encoiling bonds.

"Take aim!"

51

The six steel gun barrels were leveled. Six heads tilted as the firing squad lined their gun sights. Jessie stiffened. She was using every shred of her courage now—all the guts she had. She clamped her teeth to keep from screaming, her lips moving stiffly as she whispered a prayer. Ki felt the rope slide through his fingertips and drop, falling slack into the open grave behind his back—

And then there occurred a strange twist of fate.

From the gate that Queeg had carelessly left unlocked arose the thudding of shod hooves. The startling interruption turned the head of Blackjack Queeg, and his firing squad and other crewmen whirled around to peer down the short strip of lane. A man on horseback surged into view, at first only a fast-moving black silhouette against the gray of night. The crew hesitated a second, alarmed yet unsure. Then the rider closed near enough to be recognizable, and from the crew burst yells of surprise and warning.

"Hey, he ain't one of us!"

Jessie and Ki, catching an initial glimpse of the onrushing horseman, had to agree that he was decidedly not a Triad hand. Although in the darkness they could not see his face clearly, his clothes and slouch hat were giveaways—it was none other than Henk Willem Adriannus Van der Napier. Again.

The crew had barely raised their concerted shout before Dutch Napier opened fire with his big-bore revolver. Instantly the Triad bunch scrambled, snatching their weapons, some springing for their horses, the firing squad triggering bullets which had been meant for Jessie and Ki. And Ki, his wrists no longer tied, tackled Jessie in a springing leap, plunging them both into the open grave behind her. He tried to cushion her fall, but the sudden landing punched her breathless momentarily, dazed but at least under cover of sorts. Swiftly Ki snapped his wrist and hand bones back into place and untied her. Gasping for air, she fumbled for her pistol—

Then all hell tore loose.

Through the gate and up the lane charged the Revengers' posse, bellowing like banshees and hurling lead after Dutch Napier.

At such dead-on range, trapped in a lethal cross fire between the posse and the Triad crew, Napier should have been riddled. Fortunately, the crew had been caught napping, their aim was discombobulated, and the posse couldn't shoot straight, firing as they were from speeding horses into night shadows. Bullets ricocheted off grave markers and splintered coffins, whistling past Napier's body, uncomfortably close. But braving the gunfire without faltering, he swept through the cemetery, seeming almost to flash a grin at Jessie as his horse jumped the graves and galloped on toward the dark boulders beyond.

By then the Revengers had lost interest in chasing Napier. Suddenly finding themselves confronting a bunch of gun-wielding Triad men, they poured in like a vindictive tidal wave, turning the cemetery into an inferno of pounding hoofs, rearing horses and blazing bullets.

With howls of shock and pain, Queeg's vicious hands twisted and turned and dived behind grave markers, trying to dodge the salvos of the attacking posse. They resisted stubbornly, attempting to rally, firing back wildly. But then one crewman broke, springing onto his horse; suddenly he cried out in agony and pawed madly at his blood-spurting arm. The shock of the heavy slug almost bowled him over, but he kept his saddle, riding hell-bent for leather. His retreat set off a panicked exodus. Triad men fled headlong in every direction, vaulting into saddles or scattering on foot for the haven of the hills.

"Come back, damn you!" Blackjack Queeg shouted at his departing crew, but they were deaf to him. Heaping obscenities upon them, he spurred after. "You shitheads! Come back!"

And the Revengers' posse went storming in hot pursuit.

Climbing out of the grave, Jessie and Ki stood for a moment, nonplussed, hearing the gunfire and hoofbeats rapidly diminishing into the distance. Neither man nor beast remained in the cemetery, not even their own horses, which had bolted again in the uproar. A pungent cloud of powdersmoke clung overall like a residue of the violence.

"Well, we better scrounge up our horses," Jessie said, brushing off her clothes. "Wait—listen! A rider's coming."

"That damned Blackjack Queeg," Ki judged.

Jessie was of the same opinion. But to the utter astonishment of both, the horseman who appeared out of the cavernous night was Henk Willem Adriannus Van der Napier, leading Jessie's pinto and Ki's sorrel by their reins.

"Good evenin'," Dutch Napier said, pulling to a halt.

"Whether it's a good evening depends on your viewpoint," replied the thunderstruck Jessie. "How'd you happen to show up, like a gift from God?"

"I am a gift from God," Napier said, hurt. "Why don't you get like other folks and admit it?"

"That'll be the day. I mean how'd you show up here 'n' now?"

"Your escape was common talk back in town. I reckoned they'd reckon you'd head for Triad Ranch, being a Folgeron ally."

"Which," Ki said, "is exactly what the Revengers must've reckoned after we shook them."

Napier shrugged, grinning. "I chanced to be on the trail when they came thisaway. I guess they mistook me for a Triad ranchhand."

"Now, how could they have done that?" Jessie asked.

"Perhaps 'cause I mistook them for bandits and fired at them."

"Right. Oh, sure. Strictly a mistake," Jessie scoffed. "Well, we're here now and either the Revengers or the Triad crew or both are liable to regroup and head back here. Whether they're coming or not, I'd just as soon be going. If you'd be so kind as to hand over our mounts, Mr. Napier—Dutch?"

"Not so fast, Miss Jessie." Napier responded, making no move to relinquish the reins. "You helped me considerably yesterday. Today I evened the score back in Beyond, did I not?"

"Sure," Jessie answered warily. "And now this'll put you one up on us. Now c'mon, Dutch. We ought to make ourselves scarce before anybody shows up."

"After we strike a bargain. I help you, you help me."

"Uh-huh. And exactly how are we supposed to help you?"

"I need to get over the wall which surrounds the Triad ranch house. It's a big wall, but scaling it ain't the only problem. The outer grounds are heavily patrolled. Trying it alone, I'll get shot full of holes. But with the assistance of you two, who knows?" Again Napier shrugged. "Once inside, you'll assist me in getting a certain item. If you get it, you'll turn it over to me. And no questions asked, okay?"

"Oh, for . . . ! Very well," Jessie acquiesced. "We'll play your game. At the risk of asking you a question, what's the item we're to help you snatch with no questions asked?"

"The Tukudeka headband which Folgeron wears."

Their pinto and sorrel were given over to them by Dutch Napier, and the three rode out of the cemetery, off-trail, up the slope. Reaching into his saddlebags, Napier handed Jessie and Ki a couple of waxpaper-wrapped packages. Unwrapping them, each found inside a huge sandwich, of something that seemed like an inch-thick slice of cold roast beef, slabs of tomato and disks of Spanish onion between thick buttered bread, the sort of food served as free luncheon fare in saloons.

"I'd come to Beyond to tie on the feed bag," Napier explained, "when I discovered you two were hoose-gowed in back of Grover's Store."

"How thoughtful of you," Jessie said, wolfing her sandwich. "But say, why'd you rush out of Halfway Inn after we put you to bed?"

Napier shook an admonishing finger. "Questions ain't part of our bargain."

"Ah yes, our bargain," Ki remarked. "You sure you don't want into the Triad ranch house to grab Laverna?"

Napier's eyes darkened. "No questions, remember?"

"He knows her, all right," Jessie judged, and promptly asked another question. "What about the headband? What makes it so valuable?"

"When I have it in hand, I'll tell you. Maybe." With a wry grin, then, Napier said, "It's my turn now. What brings you to these parts, Jessie? Why'd Blackjack Queeg try to kill you and Ki?"

"No questions, remember," Jessie mocked him. "But we made a bargain. You want to get inside the ranch house and so do we. We need to talk with Winthrop Folgeron, and we've got this woman named Laverna to consider, too. As for that headband, we're willing to pick it up for you, if we can. But first we've got to get over the wall. And we'd better start figuring ways and means."

Mulling things over a moment, and keeping in mind Jessie's silence about the book in Folgeron's library, Ki spoke up: "I've an idea. It'll require that we split up, though. Dutch, do you know the country fairly well?"

Napier nodded.

"Well, we'll all go have a look-see at this wall, and figure where it might be the easiest to climb over. I'll stay there, while you take Jessie around to the other end of the ranch. Then you get off a ways and start all the hellacious fracas you can. That should bring the crew in that vicinity roaring after you."

"Yeah, they'll ride pronto," Napier agreed.

"I'm not expecting you'll be able to draw all of them, but at least their attention will be diverted away from me. About that time, I'll go over the wall. Maybe I'll run into trouble. But at least whatever men you toll to where you are won't be on my ass."

"Not a bad plan, Ki. Not good, but not bad," Napier allowed, ruminating. "Better yet, the hombre who goes over the wall shall be me. You two will be the ones raising the fuss on the opposite side."

"Nothing doing, Dutch," Jessie said flatly. "We don't know the area; you do, you said so yourself. If we're going to lead a passel of hotshot crewmen on a wild goose chase, we can't risk getting lost, cut off or box-canyoned. Don't worry; if Ki can lay his hands on the headband, he won't forget you. Or perhaps you're worried about being alone with me, hmm?"

Napier reared as if scalded, then bust out laughing. "I can see it ain't going to do no good argufyin'! Okay, Jessie, I'll play sidekick and see just how big a female caterwauler you can be."

58

Chapter 6

The terrain up to the Triad fence line had been steep, grooved bluffs and a flat rolling plain. Now, en route to the ranchstead, they crossed a land of gentle hills, streaked here and there with dunes of windblown sand. Mostly, though, it was prairie and thin soil, sometimes showing bare sandstone, and endless stretches of bluestem grass blotched with the lumpish forms of dozing cattle.

Bearing west and south, they rode silently, alertly, and approached the crest of each rise cautiously. Dutch Napier would ease ahead and reconnoiter from the ridge, making sure he saw nothing to alarm him before motioning Jessie and Ki to follow. Eventually, from just such a rimrock, they glimpsed a drift of smoke in the dim moonlit air to the southwest. This, Jessie judged, marked the ranch buildings of Winthrop Folgeron's spread, but the buildings were shut from her view by another rise of land.

Thereon the moon hid behind clouds, as though fearful of Triad Ranch, then at the last moment

59

broke clear. And thus when the three topped the final slope, there was light to bathe the buildings in the open land below them. "There, my friends, is Triad Ranch." Napier spoke with something almost like awe in his voice, and a glance was enough to show Jessie and Ki why.

They had expected the citadel of Winthrop Folgeron to be lavish, but they'd expected, too, that the layout would conform to the usual architecture of the country. Idaho was a land of log and frame. But those buildings below, reflecting in the moonlight, were made of adobe. They might have been looking at some wealthy California hacienda dating from a historic Spanish grant.

It lay between cliffs and columns of granite, in a broad valley dotted with windmills pumping water from underlying sands. With this unfailing supply of water for irrigation there were cornfields, gardens and orchards. There was a village of peon huts, each with its tiny square of garden, then many acres of sheds, corrals and bunkhouses, and finally the ranchstead proper, surrounded by a high, thick wall. Central within was the main house of many wings and patios, pantile-roofed, with huge round timbers extending out through its adobe-brick walls. It was flanked on either side by a group of smaller adobe structures, each group with its own outbuildings and corrals.

"The ranch house," Napier explained, "straddles the Idaho-Oregon border. We've come in more or less at the back. The front faces south, toward Nevada, the north boundary line of which runs east-west along a short side lane. That's why the spread is branded Triad, on ~ccount of it sitting on three locales at once."

"Mighty handy," Ki murmured, scanning the buildings. There was a sprinkling of lamplit windows, but otherwise the ranchstead bulked hard black against the softer dark of the sky. The ringing fields spread murky and indistinguishable, broken only by an occasional bobbing form of a line rider patrolling the outer perimeter. Ki was not lulled. Assuming Folgeron was as guard-happy as Napier implied, then even if the riders were lured away, he'd still have to contend with sentries posted within the walled enclosure.

"I'll hunker right here," Ki went on to say. "I should be able to hear your guns when you start your hullabaloo. Afterward, let's meet up at the Halfway Inn. It's the only spot we all know, aside from Beyond and this place."

Jessie nodded. "This place looks solid as a prison," she commented, and sighed ruefully. "It goes against my grain to let you try breaking *into* jail."

"Plus back out," Ki said. "Well, sometimes it works out the fewer there are, the better the chances."

"Nothing times nothing still equals nothing," Napier responded with a harsh laugh. "G'bye, Ki. Good luck."

Jessie and Napier rode on south along the spine of the hill, night and rock soon concealing them from Ki's sight. He waited until they were gone, then picketed his sorrel where there was cover and a smattering of forage, and chose a vantage point for himself where he could keep an eye on the ranchstead below. He settled cross-legged and purposely slowed his breathing; then, shortly, he crossed his arms and cupped his hands over his ears. He remained thus, relaxing and meditating. To a Westerner, his posture would have looked strange and uncomfortable; to a Japanese, it was a vital position for concentrating one's inner forces and reviving one's intrinsic energies, which were fundamental for health and strength. And Ki, who'd had very little rest since coming to the Devil's Playground, savored this brief respite, aware that he would probably not have another opportunity for some time to come.

Slightly more than a half-hour later, the distant rattle of gunfire shattered the thin silence of the desert country. Ki's wait was over. Stretching, limbering his muscles, he stood and listened intently. Ten minutes crept by. Far to the west, then, he spotted riders cutting diagonally overland, heading southerly in the general direction of the gunshots. After watching them vanish into the night, he collected his horse and let another ten minutes pass. Only a couple of guns had been firing; but now others began blasting away as well, and Ki smiled grimly. The chase was on.

"Here goes nothing," he said to himself, mounting.

Keeping to the rocks and cuts, Ki descended the slope and pressed on toward the Triad ranchstead, riding furtively across the bare flats until he could delve into the cover of field crops and orchards. No riders appeared—not within Ki's range of vision, anyway. Around him all was silent, save for the normal sounds of nature, the sough of a night breeze, and his own rustling progress—although far to the southwest, so many guns were blazing that it sounded as though a miniature war was being waged.

Once he reached the outer line of shanties and huts, it was easier going in some respects, harder in others. Dismounting, walking his mount by the bridle with his hat covering its muzzle, Ki could make use of the walls to hide, yet then ranchhands and guards were not as readily detected as they'd been against the open skyline. Fortunately he caught in time the noise of riders approaching along a hardpan lane, still out of sight but picking up speed as they came. He yanked his sorrel in among a series of slant-roofed tool cribs and stood breathless in the dark. Heading southwestward, eight or nine horsemen passed by at a steady gallop, bunched close, rifles across their laps.

Once they were gone, Ki moved the opposite way, ranchward, dipping behind a stretch of adobes and huts that were mostly dark, although an occasional glimmering window and muffled hum of voices denoted occupancy. Reaching a lean-to stable and corral about a hundred yards from the big wall, he left his horse in the stable with its saddle gear still on, rigged "owlhoot" style with cinches loose and bits free, hanging ready to be quickly slipped into place. Then he darted across the remaining distance, using points of cover. A parked farm wagon, a thatch of shrubbery, even the contour of a slight hump which cast a shadow, took Ki to his goal.

At the wall, he crouched in its lee. About twelve feet high, the wall was worn and grooved with age between the fieldstones of its masonry. Studying it, Ki spotted a possible foothold here, another there, a niche for his hand above that—good enough.

He started the slow, perilous climb up the ancient wall, fingers clawing for the slightest hold. A stone crumbled beneath the weight of one foot; he pressed himself flat, holding his breath, then bent tentatively in search of another anchor. Finding it, he continued to rise gradually, inch by inch.

A final flexing of muscle sent Ki over the brink, onto the broad, flat crown cemented with broken glass. His fingers spidered between the shards as he steadied himself, bringing up his legs lithely to balance catlike on his slippers. Before he could properly set himself, he glimpsed the outline of a man walking between the wall and a nearby shed. The man paced nervously, gingerly toting a Short Pattern Enfield carbine as he approached where Ki shifted delicately overhead. A tip of brittle glass snapped beneath Ki; the sound was faint, but it was enough. The man glanced upward. Ki pounced.

The man tried defending himself, but it was too late. He raised his carbine, but Ki smashed it aside as he landed on him, both knees directly in the gut. He tore the gun away, reversed it and bashed the stock against the side of the man's head. The man grunted, fell over, and lay comatose.

"Leroy!"

A man's voice, deep and gravelly, came from around the side of the shed. Ki dived for cover behind a bush, leaving the first man exactly as he'd fallen, minus his rifle. But Ki wanted to avoid shots if at all possible.

"Leroy?"

A second man trotted into view—the patrol buddy, Ki figured, attracted by the scuffle. He glanced around, not immediately spotting his partner. Ki hefted the carbine by its twenty-four–inch barrel.

"Leroy!" The second man ran to the body, kneeling to see what he could do. "Whatsa matter, pal? Too much o' that pukey whiskey we—"

Ki's swing caught the man above the temple. The man had time for a gentle gasp, his eyes rolling up to stare quizzically at Ki, before lapsing unconscious. Ki dragged him to the shed and rolled him inside, hauled the first man over to join him, then shut and latched the shed door. Their weapons he dumped behind the bush.

Then he began to steal belly-low toward the rear of the main house, advancing in circuitous stages, slipping from shed to barn, smithy to cookshack, continually on the lookout. A number of saddle horses dozed at hitch rails or in corrals, indicating there were crewmen on hand. Several men he noticed in one corral, butchering a beef; others were gathered around the wall's main entrance, peering out through its iron-barred front gates at the distant, gun-flaring night to the south. And hardcase-looking characters they were, every one of 'em, Ki decided.

Reaching the corner of the structure across from the main house, Ki drew in and listened, scanning the area. Catching nothing, he dived to the side of the house and raced down a gabled veranda. Alongside stretched a row of curtained windows, all dark save for one—which showed a dim diffusion of light through its drapes, interspersed by sudden flashes of searing brilliance. Ki circled it, keeping in shadow, and reached a patio shaded by wooden awnings. Water was carried across the patio by a masonry gutter, and it made little gurgling sounds in the dark. A balcony ran above, with French windows of second-floor bedrooms rearing behind it. Then, as Ki swept his eyes along the balcony, he saw the woman of the previous night—the terrified woman at the Halfway Inn.

She stood outlined, as before only more so, in the full-length French windows. She was dressed in a lacy gown of Spanish silk with its breast cut low. Moonlight and candle glow mixed, bringing out the soft curves of her shoulders. A black mantilla was over her head. Ki had seen many women in mantillas, but all of them had had black, glossy hair. The mantilla did something unexpected to her coils of straw-colored blond hair, gave her an extra measure of femininity.

"Laverna . . . ," Ki whispered under his breath. He wondered if she recognized him down on the patio, then realized she was gazing off at nothing in particular, and in any case he was shrouded by deep shadow.

He moved on, circling the patio, passing beneath arches and pillars in imitation of the Moorish colonnades of Old Spain. Abruptly a door opened and a splash of light was thrown across the tiling. Ki couldn't see what the door led to, but he spied a ranchhand loafing just inside, like a bored sentry. As Ki watched, a plump matron of Indian or Mexican heritage appeared in the doorway, spoke a few words to the man and stepped outside, hurrying away. Before Ki started again, another man, clad as a lowly farm laborer, approached and, speaking to the man guarding there, was admitted. A few minutes later, he, too, exited through the door.

Ki's curiosity, already piqued by the flashing light, was now thoroughly aroused. His first supposition had been that this might be the rear entrance to Winthrop Folgeron's own quarters and thus was guarded. But Folgeron's retainers would hardly be paying visits to their master this way, at this hour, and their comings and goings gave the lie to Ki's theory. Ki thought quickly, then headed around the end of the wing and returned along its back side. Here he discovered a lamp-glowing window, small-paned, which he estimated to be the window of the guarded room.

Approaching cautiously, he raised himself on tiptoe and peered inside. He could see a big room. A dozen candles burned in the holders of an ornate silver candelabra, casting light on a raised dais of polished Honduras mahogany and to the mosaic tiles of a floor that stretched away toward the room's shadowy limits, where another guard slouched in a chair next to the door. As Ki looked, the door opened and another shawled native woman entered. She crossed quickly and knelt down before the dais. She was there only a moment, praying apparently, and then she departed. But what held Ki's startled eyes was the sheet-draped figure upon the dais, candles burning smokily at its head and feet.

"Big, bearded, bald as ever," the hotel clerk had told of Winthrop Folgeron to Jessie. Such a description aptly fitted the lifeless form upon the dais, and now Ki was remembering many things and understanding them: Winthrop Folgeron writing, "I've reason to fear for my life." Blackjack Queeg snickering and saying, "I don't think Folgeron's gonna hear nothin.' "

Ki had supposed that Winthrop Folgeron had feared for his life because of the Revengers. But Folgeron hadn't died by the hands of Otis Muell and his bunch, for as late as this evening the posse had certainly not known of Folgeron's passing. And Folgeron had been dead for more than that, much more, if Ki was any judge. That waxen-fleshed corpse had the look of having been embalmed.

Disconcerted, Ki stepped back from the window. He kept going back along this side of the wing, past another set of dark, curtained windows. Finally there was a short flagstone porch with a couple of steps and a recessed doorway, the door closed. Ki paused at the door with senses keen, but he saw nothing outside and didn't hear anything from within. Not surprisingly, the door proved to be locked. Hunkering down on the stoop, Ki removed from his vest a knife known as a *navaj* its six-inch blade the thinnest and most pliant of the daggers he carried. As he had hoped, it slid easily between the doorjamb and faceplate. Levering and picking, he cautiously snicked back the latch bolt and pushed open the door.

No movement. No sign of anyone. Satisfied, Ki eased inside and shut the door quietly behind him. As his eyes adjusted to the darkness, he found that he was standing in a large pantry. Directly ahead was a kitchen, unoccupied, though its clutter of foodstuffs and utensils showed that it was in constant use. He passed through to the next room, a dining room with a table capable of seating a platoon with elbow space to spare, aglitter under the crystal drops of a tiered chandelier. Ki hesitated, bird-dogged by apprehensions, even though he continued to hear nothing. Nothing at all . . .

That sort of worried him—hearing nothing at all.

Edging on nonetheless, Ki entered what had to be the main reception room of the sprawling ranch house. It had the vast, echoing presence of a museum, with Indian artifacts displayed in glass cases, on tables and the walls—tribal masks, wood and stone carvings, beadwork, tools and weaponry—and a ceiling-high totem pole erected in the center. One one side were closed double doors; on the other rose a bannistered staircase to the second floor; and directly ahead extended a corridor lined with doors, all shut.

Ki was angling for the double doors, to see if they led to Folgeron's library, when bright light suddenly flared from under the door at the end of the corridor. Changing direction, he eased down the corridor and flattened against the door, listened intently, then peered through its keyhole.

From what little he could see of the room beyond, it seemed that up on each of the side walls there was a bracket lamp, and the low flames of the lamps provided the only illumination. There were thick drapes of an intense scarlet covering the window, and shelving lined with cans of chemicals and bottles of brown-hued glass. Near one corner was a dry-plate view camera mounted on a tripod, with a flash-powder holder next to it. Behind the camera, a photographer had his head ducked under its black gossamer focus cloth.

The camera was aimed at the center of the room, where Ki caught the white glimmer of a background screen used for posing purposes. Posing! That, Ki perceived, stifling a gasp, was an understatement. In front of the screen was a garden bench on which was seated a naked man. Straddling his thighs was a nude woman, her head resting on his shoulder. She was facing the camera, belly sucked in, long black hair spilling over her pink shoulders, legs wide to display the man buried long and hard within her loins.

"Hold it!" the photographer ordered. "Don't move."

The man on the bench groaned as he strove to obey.

Emerging from under the focus cloth, the photographer struck a match. "Hold it right like that!"

By the matchlight, Ki saw that the photographer was a lanky man with a high, wrinkled forehead and sparse graying hair. His expression was a study in carnal pleasure, his eyes bulging and his mouth agape, almost slavering. Then the photographer put the match to the flash powder, and as the powder ignited with a dazzling burst, he squeezed the bulb of the camera's shutter mechanism.

Leaning away, Ki rubbed his momentarily blinded eye, then looked again. Now the photographer was busily changing plates and barking orders at the woman. She was maneuvering around, her back to the camera so that her arching pink buttocks seemed poised over the man for a downward stroke. But, Ki had to admit, there was no percentage in spying through the keyhole with his lower jaw flapping, so reluctantly he unglued his eye and retreated back along the corridor.

The double doors were unlocked. He inched one open and slipped through, finding that his hunch had been right and that this was Winthrop Folgeron's library.

Library! Hell, it was the den of a sybarite, of a man who knew what he liked and surrounded himself with its emblems. Sitting on tables and on the many bookshelves were prurient statues of wood and ivory, nude figurines carved in sensuous detail. Between the shelves, the walls were hung with erotic art work—mezzotints and oils, washes and watercolors, and framed photographs showing men and women joined in classical love postures.

The choice of books proved no less boggling. As he perused the titles, searching for the third book from the left on the fourth shelf from the floor nearest the door, Ki ran across the infamous *Kama Sutra,* an illustrated *Nouvel Album Erotique,* De Sade's *Justine,* and the collected poems of Paul Verlaine. Finally, wedged between *The Sins of Sister Angela* and Baudelaire's *To a Courtesan,* Ki located the book in which Folgeron had left written instructions, the innocent sounding *Magistrate System of Attica, 330 B.C.*

It was a heavy volume, written in Latin. Flipping the pages, Ki came upon a wax-sealed envelope which apparently contained many sheets of flimsy paper, and he drew in his breath triumphantly. He was about to run his thumb under the flap when there arose a furious clamor out by the wall. The sentries! They had either been discovered in the shed or had regained consciousness and broken out. Boots were pounding close about the ranch house— the feet of Triad gunmen drawn by the commotion.

Ki was surrounded, trapped inside, cut off from escape.

Chapter 7

Book in hand, Ki ran out of the library.

He padded across the museum-like reception room and went up the stairs, keeping close to the wall so that the treads wouldn't creak. At the second floor landing, he glanced both ways; nobody was in the hallway—yet. Like a fleeting shadow, he hastened down the hall counting bedroom doors, hoping for better results this time than he'd had last night at Halfway Inn. Pausing at one particular door, fingers on the knob, he failed to hear anything through the thick, solid panel. He knocked guardedly, then opened the door enough to slip in, shutting it quickly behind him.

For the first time Ki got a really good look at the woman called Laverna. Up close, she appeared more petite in slippers and gown than she had seemed from the angle of the balcony window. Petite and feminine and vulnerable. And now he was certain of what he'd begun to suspect down at the patio— that he'd seen her years before, that he knew who she was. But there was no sign of recognition in her eyes, no apparent memory of him from the inn. Her eyes grew big and afraid, the markings of a scream growing.

Hastily Ki raised a finger to his lips in a quieting gesture. "I'm a friend," he said in a low, urgent voice. "I'm the guy you signaled from the window at Halfway Inn last night."

Recognition struck her. "You found the message in the dust of the windowsill?" she asked in a throaty whisper, a whiskey-and-cigarette velvety purr.

"I found it, Laverna . . . Miss Laverna Pegaso."

"How . . . ?"

"The San Francisco Opera. I saw you as Lucia, in Donizetti's *Lucia di Lammermoor*. The reviews raved, as I recall, about the auspicious performance by soprano Laverna Pegaso, singing one of the most demanding dramatic coloratura roles in opera. Something like that, anyway."

"That was ages ago. A fine memory, Mister . . . ?"

"Ki. Just Ki."

"Ah yes, the companion to Miss Starbuck."

"You knew it was us last night?"

"I had hoped, when I saw you. Winthrop—Mr. Folgeron had told me of writing Miss Starbuck, and then more recently, of hearing back from her." Laverna moved closer to Ki, so close that she brushed against him. "Yes, you've a fine memory, Ki. The next season I caught catarrh of the throat from that beastly Bay fog and had to retire. Ever since I've been, well, with Winthrop. He was a high flyer back then, he was. He enjoyed the finer things in life, and I wanted someone interesting and a little different."

"Very different, by the look of things," Ki said meaningfully, glancing around her bedroom. He paid little attention to the walnut wardrobe or the chair and small writing desk; most bedrooms had those, more or less. Rather, he concentrated on a set of etchings which showed two men enjoying the embraces of five (count 'em) unclad females in various postures and deviations.

"Well, Winthrop started gathering up such bits of erotica, here and there," she responded with a blasé shrug. "I never understood his interest. After all, a man and a woman have only so many working parts. But he'd keep adding to them, off and on."

"Joke, Laverna?"

"What?"

"Adding to them off and on, I mean. It's no joke, though, that Folgeron is dead. I saw him laid out downstairs."

"Winthrop shall be buried as soon as a fancy coffin I've ordered for him has arrived. Fortunately, the man he'd put in charge of his Indian collection is a taxidermist and knows the art of embalming."

"Who's the gent continuing Folgeron's fig-leaf photography?"

"Oh, that'd be Winthrop's attorney, Enoch Hyde."

Jessie, Ki recollected, had mentioned that the headband-wearing imposter back in Beyond had referred to an Enoch Hyde. Hyde was the city-slick shyster who'd helped Folgeron forge his stolen empire. For that matter, Hyde resembled the phony Folgeron described by Jessie. Damn convenient of

Hyde to be here, carrying on now.

"Excuse my asking," Ki said, on a sudden suspicion, "but did the embalmer patch up a bullet hole or so in Folgeron?"

"Winthrop died of natural causes," Laverna assured with a demure smile; her hand reached, and as if by accident, her long, aristocratic fingers touched the front of Ki's vest. "True, he died with his boots on. But that's all he had on, I can testify to that."

"I see. His flesh was willing, but his spirit was weak, eh?"

"Let's just say he came and he went."

"Why is Hyde—"

Before Ki could finish his question, he was interrupted by a dull roar of voices and the trampling of boots up the stairs and along the hallway. Laverna blanched.

"Hyde's on his way here! Quick, he mustn't find you!"

During their brief conversation, Ki had been leafing through the book he carried, hunting for any more documents stashed between its pages. There were no others, and now, thrusting the one envelope he'd already found inside his vest, he dropped the book on the desk and looked for someplace to conceal himself. Going out through the window was out of the question; Triad crewmen could be heard trooping across the patio below, sure to spot him on the balcony. Desperately he dived into the walnut wardrobe. Wedging back among Laverna's hanging clothes, he drew the door almost shut, holding it with

76

the tip of one of his daggers, for there was no inside knob to latch it completely closed.

He was none too soon, either. For a moment later the door of her bedroom burst open, and Enoch Hyde rushed in. He was brandishing a revolver, as were the handful of henchmen behind him, most of whom continued on along the hall, though a couple hesitated at the threshold of m'lady's boudoir, unsure whether to follow Hyde inside. Hyde took care of that by slamming the door in their faces.

"What," Laverna demanded, "is the meaning of this?"

"I wish I knew, I wish I knew," Hyde growled distractedly, peering about. "A gang of raiders attacked out in the south forty, and now apparently some maniac is on the loose here in the compound. You haven't seen anybody, have you?"

"Don't be absurd."

Hyde muttered something and stuck his revolver behind his belt. Or so it seemed to Ki, who couldn't see more than the back of Hyde from his cramped vantage. Hyde paused, indecisive, legs wide and hands on his hips. Finally he lifted his broad shoulders in a shrug of unwilling helplessness and looked around one more time, as if trying to find some excuse to stay. He did, apparently, picking up the copy of *Magistrate System of Attica, 330 B.C.* that Ki had left on the desk.

"I'd never have guessed you to be a scholar, m'dear," Hyde remarked. "You've chosen a rather ponderous tome."

"The heavier the book, the sooner I'll sleep," Laverna retorted. "Good night, Mr. Hyde."

"M'dear, I've told you enough times not to call me Mr. Hyde. Do you know how it makes me feel when you call me that? I feel like a usurer in a black silk hat come to foreclose the mortgage. Please, call me Enoch." He had an oily personality, and he was putting it on for Laverna, trying to sound earnest as he stood looking down at her. "Why do you build such a fortress around yourself? You know I care for you."

"Indeed."

"Yes. And I'm vain enough to think you care for me, if you'd be truthful with yourself. This ranch has become an obsession with you. Holding it together, a monument to the glory of Winthrop Folgeron. Well, I'll tell you this, Miss Pegaso, there is only one way to make Triad a great brand, and that is by business methods. Yes, sharp business methods. Think of what *we* could do with Triad Ranch—together."

She said quietly, "You're asking me to marry you?"

"For the tenth time, I am asking you to be my wife. You've managed to put me off before, but I think I'm due for an answer. A yes or no."

"No."

The word was soft as a cat's paw, but it struck Hyde hard. He started to turn, checked himself, and took a stride toward her. He said, "You talk about Triad being your trust, about you saving it, and yet you turn away the one man who could save it for you."

She laughed, and her voice had a whiplike taunt. "Now who comes like a black-hat banker, Mr. Hyde?"

"No!" he said. "I'm not a banker. I'm not a lawyer right now, either. I'm a man, and you're a beautiful woman." His hands reached and closed, fingers sinking deep in the bare flesh of her shoulders.

"Let me go!" she hissed, twisting from side to side.

"No, m'dear. You can't play cat with me any longer."

She was unexpectedly strong. Her hands found his wrists, tore herself free, but Hyde seized her again, arms closing around her back. For a second her face was pressed against his chest, eyes peering over his shoulder at Ki, who was on the verge of leaping out of the wardrobe, damn the consequences. She shook her head, begging Ki not to intervene, while simultaneously she kneed Hyde in the balls. Hyde snapped back. He reeled, clutching his groin, and went down writhing. His right hand clawed for his revolver—

"No!" It was the voice of Laverna, adamant and determined. She held a Wesson .22 hideaway pistol. "It is cocked and aimed at your heart. I do not wish to pull the trigger, but I will. Get out."

Hyde climbed to his feet, stood for a moment facing Laverna, chest rising and falling with deep breathing. Strands of his gray hair had fallen across his face, and he fingered them out of the way. "M'dear—"

"Get out."

Hyde still fingered his sparse hair, his long face savage from frustration. He hissed a vile word through clenched teeth, turned, and strode out the door, whipping it shut behind him. Laverna released the hammer to safety, lifted the hem of her gown and slipped the small pistol into a frilly leg garter. Ki did not emerge at once, being not so quick to believe Hyde was gone for good. Even when Laverna opened the wardrobe door, he waited a moment just to make sure. Then, about to come out, he caught the sound of footsteps again, approaching along the hall.

There was a deferential knock on the door and a crewman entered, bearing a goblet of brandy. "Compliments of Mist' Hyde," he said, setting the goblet on the desk. "It's to help you sleep if your readin' keeps you awake."

"How thoughtful," Laverna said, with the merest hint of sarcasm, and extended the book to the man. "You can take this back to Mr. Hyde with my thanks. Tell him I made a mistake. The only Latin I understand is Pig Latin."

"Yes'm, soon's I'm off duty."

"Off duty?"

"Yes'm. I'm to stay just outside here, guardin' you against any an' all intruders." With a sheepish grin, the man took the book and left the room, closing the door after him.

Ki eased out of the wardrobe, wondering whether Hyde had grown suspicious or homicidal. If so, his own danger had really just begun, and so too had Laverna's. She faced what—an assassin in the night? Perhaps. A poison or sleeping potion in the

80

brandy to leave her completely at the mercy of Hyde . . . ?

"That horrid man," Laverna murmured, shuddering, rubbing her bare arms as though chilled to the bone. "I'm in a tough spot, Ki, and I'm all mixed up. I don't know what to do. Help me, please."

Ki didn't answer right away. Suddenly, after the raw violence, everything had changed. He noticed how the toes of her slippers barely peeked beneath the cascades of her gown, smelled the fragrance of her perfumed skin, heard the liquid music of the water running across the patio in its masonry gutter. The moment had a dreamlike quality he did not want to disturb. But she had asked, begged, for his assistance—

Ki picked up the brandy and sniffed it. He couldn't be sure if it had been doctored or not, but what the hell. Leaning forward, he whispered in her ear. She nodded, took the goblet from him and walked to the door, while he faded back into the shadows. She cracked open the door, and Ki overheard her speak to the crewman posted outside.

"I'm so relieved you're protecting me. What's your name?"

"Me? Why, er, Tucker, Elvis Tucker."

"Well, Elvis Tucker, here's my glass of brandy to make your vigil less tedious. I've had enough for one night."

A hairy hand extended, grabbed the goblet. There was a chugalug swallowing sound. "Thanks, ma'am," the man belched, returning the empty goblet.

"My pleasure," Laverna said, and closed the door.

Joining her, Ki again whispered in her ear to avoid being overheard. "If there's anything wrong with the brandy, the guard will be dead out or flat dead in about thirty minutes. Do you have any clothes handy? Clothes for the trail?"

She nodded, scrutinizing him with her deep, luminous eyes.

"Pile into them. And hurry."

"Why? We have half an hour, don't we?" She untied the ribbon at the throat of her gown and then began to unhook the little clasps of the bodice. Her chin was raised and her uptilted face was yearning. "I need you, Ki. I'm all alone. I don't have anybody to turn to and I'm lonely and I'm very grateful for your help. Personally very grateful."

Ki was growing interested, but he was also growing worried about playing her game. He wondered how far she'd tease, how far was *too* far, and he didn't care to face any more uproar than he had to tonight. "Laverna, you don't have to—"

"I know. I want to." She laughed a little and opened the rest of the clasps. "Let's not quarrel. Let's put off the silent minutes until it's time and be friends." Shrugging her shoulders, she slipped the gown off and let it blossom around her feet, baring smooth, slightly freckled skin, pointed breasts topped by raspberry-sized nipples, and a plump pudendum, with lips accentuated by a thin line of velvety curls.

Then, doffing her slippers and pistol-packing garter, she pressed her naked body against Ki and kissed him for a long, burning moment. Ki responded with enthusiasm, kissing her back, feeling her lips clinging hungrily, her fingers trailing along his thigh, unbuttoning his fly. Then she was bending over, pushing his pants down. And all the while, Ki kept thinking he was a damn fool for allowing this, but what the hell, either the guard wouldn't notice and they had the time, or the guard would and it was too late now anyway.

"Ohh, are you hung," Laverna cooed when he was fully exposed, and she straightened to embrace him, smothering anything he might have said.

Aroused, Ki broke away from her clasp, hastening to be rid of his clothes. Laverna stepped back and stretched out nude on her bed, watching him strip with that vacant, burnt expression some women get when they're ready for sex. She was breathing hard, as though there wasn't enough air in the room, when, naked, Ki lay alongside her on the bed and embraced her. His hands moved impulsively, spreading tenderly across her flat stomach and up over her swollen breasts. Trembling from his touch, she shuddered and gripped him, pulling him, urging his hand to slide between her legs and along her sleek inner thighs. Her hips slackened, widening to allow him access while she kept murmuring in a low, passionate voice: "Take me, take me, fill me . . ."

But Ki was not ready to take her. He dallied first in the delights of sexual foreplay. He licked the curve of her neck and the tiny lobes of her ears, then moved lower, nuzzling and kissing one breast at a time. His groin pressed against her pubic bone, and he began pumping his jutting erection along the

83

sensitive crevice between her thighs, yet never quite penetrating her.

Laverna opened and closed her eyes, gasping and whimpering. Her buttocks jerked and quivered, her legs rolling and squirming until they were splayed out on the coverlet, one of her feet pushing up against the iron frame of the bed. "Don't tease me, Ki," she mewled, panting harshly. "Put it in, oh, please put it in." In a frenzy, she reached between them and placed his taunting member against the opening of her moist sheath, prodding Ki into herself with her own trembling fingers.

"Now," she sighed breathlessly, swallowing the whole of him up inside her belly as she arched her back off the bed. "Now, *con brio!*"

Crooning, Laverna kicked her feet out and locked clawing arms and legs firmly around Ki's impaling body. He felt her eager muscles tightening smoothly around him in a pressuring action of their own, and he set his mind to the dangerous ecstasy of the moment. Tighter she wrapped her limbs, deeper she sank her fingernails, rhythmically matching Ki's building tempo as his body pounded hers against the mattress.

A creaky bed in a house full of killers, Ki thought dizzily, was not the ideal spot for such frantic sport. But that was about all he thought, as they panted in concentration, pummeling each other with ever-quickening strokes. He pumped into her until she was a hot river, until he could feel her not knowing or caring who or what that thing inside her was, just letting it drive up and down inside her with lavish fanaticism.

Abruptly Laverna cried out in release, her fist stuffed into her mouth to stifle her high-pitched sounds of wanton ecstasy. Clenching his teeth, Ki felt his orgasm welling up, triggered by the gripping convulsions of her spasms. He flowed deep inside her, flooding her. She splayed her legs wide, arching up with pressing force to hold all of his surging passion, until, with a final convulsion, she lay still, satiated.

"Never with Winthrop," she sighed blissfully. "Never like that."

After a moment, Ki withdrew gently and stretched out beside her, his hand resting on her thigh. At last he rose and dressed, then padded silently to the door. Cracking the door ajar, he glanced out cautiously.

Elvis Tucker was fast asleep, his breathing deep and steady.

"The brandy was drugged, okay," Ki said, returning to Laverna.

Languidly she stirred from the bed and delved into the wardrobe. A few minutes later she was ready to go, clad in a black silk shirt with silver spangles. Around her waist was a heavy belt studded with silver and gold, cinched tight to hold her forked skirt of Spanish leather. Actually it was more chaparejos than skirt, designed to turn the harsh thorns and burrs of the desert country. She buckled on a holstered revolver, a Bisley .38–40, wearing it in a peculiar manner, high on the left side, its barrel slanting almost horizontally.

Carrying her boots in hand, Laverna snuck out with Ki into the hall. Quietly Ki closed the door after them, careful not to disturb the snoring crewman slumped on his butt against the wall. Laverna motioned for him to follow her, but he placed a restraining hand on her arm.

"Which room is Enoch Hyde's?" he whispered.

"Four doors down. This way."

Silently they glided the short length to the door to Hyde's quarters. It gave to Ki's touch. Laverna didn't know what Ki had in mind, but trusting his judgment, she kept nervous watch in the hall while he stealthily entered the room.

Moonlight trickled feebly through a grilled window. Ki could make out furniture of carved woods, massive and expensive. The bed was a cavernous canopy affair, and on the walls were pictures and a bas-relief or two of the lurid sort he'd seen in the library and Laverna's rooms. Near the bed was a large oak dresser fitted with a shaped bevel plate mirror, and from a hook atop one side of the mirror frame dangled a headband. Ki drew a long breath as he lifted the headband off the hook, seeing that it was Indian-fashioned of leather and beadwork, matching the description Jessie had given. For want of a better means of carrying it, he placed it upon his head and returned to the hall.

Laverna gazed in surprise at the headband. "Why'd you go to all the trouble of getting that thing?"

"Don't know, yet," Ki replied enigmatically. "Let's move."

Accompanying Laverna on along the carpeted hall, uneasiness was an icy-footed centipede crawling up Ki's spine. He was willing enough to let her do the leading; she knew the ranch far better than he did. Besides, she moved with long swinging strides, her skirt snug and jouncing fetchingly. Reaching a small rear landing, they descended a narrow back staircase, hugging the wall, testing each step with gingerly caution before trusting their weight to it. At the bottom, they padded across to a small side door, and then they were outside, where Laverna took a moment to pull on her boots. They were tiny boots, intricately stitched and inlaid.

"My horse," she said, in answer to his question, "is corralled at the end of the far wing."

They stuck to the thick shadows, hurrying for the corral that was, Ki realized, across the Nevada line. He tuned his ears to the night. The far-off gunfire had quieted, either because of distance or because the chase was over, one way or another. A few lights glowed yellow in the main house and adjacent outbuildings, and from several directions came agitated voices. Hopefully they wouldn't be spotted, or Laverna discovered to be missing, until they were gone . . . but Ki couldn't count on it.

At the corral gate, he distinguished the vague shapes of animals inside. Laverna gave a soft whistle. It was answered by a low nicker of welcome, but her horse did not come to meet her. She slid open one pole of the gate and they entered. Her horse—a piebald mare—was found tied to a feed rack under a long, open-front tack shed to one side. Her saddle gear was stowed in the shed, put away there by the crewman who'd last tended her mount.

Running his eye over the other horses, Ki selected a splotched paint. Hastily he saddled, explaining to Laverna that if all went well, he wanted to switch to his own sorrel as soon as they'd gotten outside the wall. Then, nerves screwed tight, they led their mounts toward the gate, walking carefully, watching each step to keep their footfalls from sounding on loose stone.

"Closed for the night," Ki observed, peering ahead. It wasn't only that the gate was shut and some men were lounging there; this whole layout made him feel edgy. It was as grim as the limitless desert surrounding it. Dipping into his vest, he retrieved the sealed letter of Folgeron's that he'd taken from the book. "Here," he said, handing the document to Laverna. "We've made it this far; question is whether we'll make it any farther. If we get separated, keep these for me—"

"Shh!" she cautioned. "Someone's outside the gate, opening it!"

Ki's eyes narrowed. "Blackjack Queeg!" He wrenched the headband from his own head and placed it on Laverna's. "We're going to have to rush that gate. If you get through, wait for me at Halfway Inn, where we were last night. Got it?"

"Yes, but—"

"Good! And hang onto those papers meanwhile!" He slapped hard at her horse, which bolted forward, heading toward the opened gate. "And keep moving, whatever else!" he called as she went charging through, bowling men aside and nearly riding down an astonished Blackjack Queeg.

After her, at a hard gallop, raced Ki.

"Wha' th' fuck!" Queeg raged, stumbling for his balance. And then sounded the pungent discharge of a gun from some henchman close by, an orange tongue of flame lancing out, followed by another bellow from Queeg. "Watch it! Don't hit the bitch! Get him! Get the squint-eyed bastard!"

Hunching low over the horse's withers, Ki neither saw nor sensed the crouched figure of a long-haired breed up on the side portal of the gate. As Ki came storming by, the waiting man came hurtling down, agile and deadly as a catamount, to land on his back. The man's upraised knife cut a downward arc. Staggered under the unexpected impact of his attacker's body, Ki glimpsed the blade glitter in the starlight as it flashed over his shoulder. Quicker than thought, he threw up one arm and blocked it. With a spontaneous heave of desperation, he flung the man from his back—flung him sideward and down.

The knife wielder struck the ground hard on his back, but not before his gripping hand unseated Ki from horseback. Tumbling, Ki landed atop the breed, who scissored his legs around Ki and tried to wrench free his knife hand for a killing thrust. Their bodies oddly entwined, they thrashed furiously about on the ground.

Ki heard the thud of boots rushing in. He saw shadowy figures close about them, like wolves surrounding their prey, and heard the jabber of yells and curses. Against the stars he beheld the swift swing of a gun barrel lashing down and instinctively wrenched himself to one side. The breed's head took the blow of that down-swinging gun; his muscles went slack; the knife, gripped in his twisted hand above his own chest, plunged downward under Ki's shifting weight. Its keen point slipped neatly between the breed's ribs, and the long blade buried itself to the hilt in his heart. And in that same swift movement, Ki untangled himself and rolled clear.

Before he could gain his feet, however, a boot thudded into him. The melee instantly became a whirling, panting dogfight, shrouded in sinister gloom. An unseen blow landed on Ki's skull and pain fogged his brain, while his reflexes fought blindly for his life. Arms encircled his knees, and a man's body weight pinned down his legs, anchoring him fast.

"Got 'im!" the man shouted. "Bash in his head!"

"I'll blow it off!" cried an excited voice. "Stand clear!" It was Blackjack Queeg. He was trying to locate Ki's head with the muzzle of his revolver.

Half-dazed, Ki felt the muzzle against his ear. As if stung by a scorpion, he flung up his head. The gunshot was deafening. Ki fumbled in his vest for one of his daggers, clutching its haft, twisting to break free of the man on his legs. Another gun barrel slashed at his head. He sensed rather than saw it coming, and his limber body jackknifed forward. His free hand found a man's head in his lap; his fingers fastened in its hair. The man squirmed, uttered a hoarse outcry as Ki desperately drove the dagger into his back. But the man's clutching arms did not loosen; they tightened in a grip of death.

Choked with dust, dazed with pain, Ki lost hope of ever regaining his feet, lost hope of ever breaking through that circle of swinging guns and stomping boots. He caught one boot in the crook of his arm, reached high his other arm and brought his knife across the imprisoned leg, cutting deep. With a horrified oath, the man tried to pull away. Ki held fast and slashed again.

With a wild scream, the man swung his gun at Ki's upturned face. Ki met the blow with his dagger. The man's wrist struck square across the point. His grip loosened, his gun dropping, clouting Ki in the eye. Letting go of the man's leg, Ki grasped the gun, settled its butt into his hand. With other boots and guns raining blows upon him, he began shooting blindly upward among his attackers.

Pandemonium erupted. The Triad crew fell back, as some of his aimless shots drove home. A horse screamed, struck by a glancing slug. Ki exerted his last strength, broke free of those tight arms about his legs, and staggered to his knees. Around him pounded boots and hoofs as frantic men and spooked horses bunched and milled, alike in their stampeding. The gate entrance became a blot of whirling dust and rushing forms. One struck Ki and he went down heavily, stunned and asprawl.

For him the fight was over.

Chapter 8

Earlier that same night, while Ki was preparing to sneak into the Triad ranchstead, Henk Willem Adriannus Van der Napier grinned at Jessie and whispered, "Nice night for driving cattle." It was the first comment he had made since they'd left Ki on the ridge, other than cautioning Jessie to silence by saying, "We could run into company, if we ain't heedful."

No company here. Not enough cover down on the flats. They had kept to the cover of the slope for as long as possible, riding far south, then risked descending westward to the valley floor. From there they'd approached the outskirts of the Triad range, trying to conceal themselves among boulders and along dry-wash channels while scanning the rolling acres for guards. Finally, emerging from a defile, they now found themselves in what the Mexicans call a *vallecito*, a pocket valley sprouting bucknut, sage and patches of galleta grass.

Jessie counted thirty steers grazing there.

"Look at 'em," Dutch Napier said with a twist of his mouth. "Plump an' peaceful and maybe their tails braided. By damn they'll have some o' that taller run off 'em before the hour is up."

"And a pack of Triad riders will wind up a lot leaner, too," Jessie said, drawing her saddle carbine. "Fine idea of yours, Dutch. Nothing like a little cattle rustling and stampeding to get crewmen in a hot-roaring lather."

"Don't set things off yet, Jessie. There's something I want to do first." Slipping on a pair of old ropers' gloves, Napier uncoiled his saddle rope, fashioned one end into a bowline for a lariat and tied the other end to his saddlehorn. "One thing we can't do is lead 'em to Halfway Inn. Let's stick tight and head southwest, toward the Santa Rosa Mountains."

Jessie nodded agreement, surveying the sweep of the *vallecito* and surrounding rises for sign of Triad hands patrolling or riding herd.

Picking out the likeliest steer, Napier rushed swiftly, spurs raking. It was young, older than a calf but still a good year from full growth; and it was relatively near, about forty yards away. Startled, the steer clambered upright and pivoted to run, but Napier's cagey roan cut and blocked it, allowing him to close in before tossing his loop. He snagged the steer over its horns from behind, then flipped the rope to one side, while his horse veered to the other. The steer dropped, its hind legs wrenched out from under it. Napier lit down, and as his roan held the catch-rope taut, he hog-tied the steer with piggin strings.

Jessie watched perplexed as, unsheathing a bowie-style knife, Napier crouched over the struggling steer and studied its flanks as though hunting for iron brands. Evidently he found one. Slicing around the brand, he peeled a ragged square of hide from the warm meaty flesh as quickly but as gently as possible. His field surgery was crude and not very humane, but she also knew the wound would eventually scar over, and his only alternative was to kill the steer. It was not his to kill . . . or was it? What Napier was up to was the sort of thing done when checking for blotted brands, as though even he wasn't sure exactly whose steer it was.

Napier released the steer, which reared to its feet, loud and mournful. Cattle nearby were taking alarm, scrambling up, bawling. In turn they were arousing other cattle farther around, querulous lowing spreading out like ripples in a pond. Pocketing the strip of cowhide in his saddlebag and recoiling his rope, Napier signaled for Jessie to head around one side of the herd while he swung around the other.

Charging, Jessie and Napier fired into the air, boogering the cattle into motion. They were well-fed cattle, but still wild as buffalo after having spent their lives in desert brush country. There was no trouble moving them. Some of them set off at a lope, and the running of those started the rest. Their hoofs became louder as the whole herd in the *vallecita* scattered, bellowing.

A Triad rider appeared, trying to stem them. Others followed him—the night herders, just awakened and groggily confused. More men came into view, bunched in the manner of patrolling guards. Gunshots knifed the dark. Jessie could see the powder flashes among the oncoming men. Flame spurted from twenty points, centering on her and Napier as they angled in to merge together again, riding southwesterly. Range was short, but dust, darkness and swift movement gave them a chance to escape.

Twisting around in his saddle, Napier levered and fired his carbine one-handedly. Far back a man cried in pain. A salvo of answering shots came from the Triad riders as they stormed in feverish pursuit. Most of their slugs went wild, though one fanned close by Jessie, and another sent spatters of lead as it glanced from a rock in front of her horse's feet.

The whine of lead only seemed to act on Napier like heady wine, making his nostrils flare and his lips stretch in a mirthless grin. He led them across rising ground to a narrow canyon formed by a dry wash. Its bottom seemed to be impenetrable from thorn, but a trail opened at the final instant and he followed it, guiding them through night shadow, making every unpredictable turn as it took zigzag courses up the rocky side and down again, until finally it reached a sort of rolling summit from which the valley could be viewed in the wan moonlight.

Blind gunfire and cussing howls tagged them, as, behind and below, the Triad riders blundered through the thorny thickets. Their frustrated rage acted on Napier like the bullets had just acted on him, appealing to his wild nature, provoking cynical laughter. After a moment, holding his roan on a tight rein, he nudged it on, forging a slow hundred yards along the canyon brush with Jessie a pace behind. Huge sandstone boulders had fallen from above, blocking the way, and they had to swing far out in avoiding them.

Gunfire was rising from up the canyon, each shot sounding like a dozen as it bounded from the rock walls. Now and then their eyes caught flashes way back along the ledge trail, pursuers still dogging their path with stubborn fury. The rifle echo prevented them from detecting the oncoming approach of a lone crewman, and it was Napier's roan that gave them warning. It made a twitch, a sideward movement. Napier turned in the saddle, motioning to Jessie with his carbine, then leveled in on target, detecting the shadow of the horsemen who had apparently materialized out of nowhere.

He was so close, so close that the moon, slanting down between the rock-ribbed walls, gave an instant impression of his face: young, perhaps nineteen, with unshaven rubbery cheeks and a loose, corrupt mouth. His horse spied Napier and Jessie and whinnied. The man came around swiftly, his revolver drawn, but for the second he held it with the barrel angled toward the sky. He looked into the bore of Napier's .44–40, and the beginning of a snarl died on his face and his mouth slacked a little in fear and consternation.

Napier humped his roan up beside the man. "Toss me your iron, amigo."

The young man sat there undecided. Fear and

rebellion clashed in the depths of his eyes. Napier eased back the hammer of his .44–40. Beneath him, the roan was restless. Napier had to keep an iron grip on the reins with his left hand. Despite the small jerkings of his mount, Jessie noticed, Napier's revolver never wavered out of line with the rider's chest.

"I'm not waiting all night," Napier warned.

"Lemme tell you somet'in'," the man said, with false braggadocio. "Don't stick around. Keep on ridin'. You've picked the wrong bunch to hassle."

"I stay where I please," Napier snapped, his voice chill. "Save your threats for a woman. That seems to be more Triad's style. Now, throw it here and do it nice, lest you want me to burn powder."

Flushing, the man bit off a curse. His fingers relaxed about the handle of his pistol, and then he worked them so that he held the pistol with the cylinder in his palm. He tossed it, and Napier released the reins long enough to catch the weapon with his left hand. He shoved it into his waistband and took up the lines again as the roan shied nervously. The drumming hoofbeats of the Triad pursuers were gaining, growing uncomfortably close now.

"Get down and start hoofin'," Napier ordered, and as the man grudgingly dismounted, he added, "tell your pals they're on the wrong trail. Tell 'em there's nothin' here but a slug for each one of 'em if they don't turn back." He aimed at the man's feet and pulled the trigger. The bullet made the man jump in the air. "Hurry up, amigo, before I change my mind and plug you through your heart."

The man turned hurriedly on his heel. His spurs made small, protesting noises as he trotted by Napier and Jessie, back up the trail the way they had come. The instant he was around the next crag, out of sight, Napier punched the spent shell from his Colt and inserted a fresh load. Then he and Jessie urged their horses back far enough so that they could peer around the crag. The man was running with his right hand held up in a signal halting the oncoming riders.

The first handful of riders were in a tight galloping knot, then four more, and plenty of others strung out behind. Napier and Jessie were close enough, and the moon was just bright enough—they could have dropped one or two with carbines, but there was no point in that. After Napier murmured to Jessie, they waited till the man reached the riders, then threw shots in the ground right in front of the oncoming horses.

The horses spooked, rearing, bucking, careening against each other. The man squalled in fright and threw himself to the ground to avoid tromping by one of the wheeling steeds. The riders fought to regain control, straightening out, most reversing at a gallop along the trail toward the bottom of the canyon, those in front colliding with those at the back.

Napier reined his roan around. "Let's go."

"You think this'll stop them?" Jessie scoffed.

"Hell, no. It'll only goad 'em after us," Napier

answered, riding the roan over to where the crewman's cow pony stood with trailed reins. "That's the gen'ral idea." He clapped the cow pony on the rump and it went off at a run. "Now, let's get out of here while we can!"

★

Chapter 9

They spurred their horses on along the narrow ledge trail. A ragged barrage of shots came sniping after them from the canyon. The ground ahead began to rise again, and they slowed their mounts for the climb through the mountain and plateau country of the Devil's Playground. Every so often Jessie sensed Napier studying her, yet whenever she glanced at him he was looking down at his horse's ears.

Presently they came out on a high shelf that afforded them a dizzying view of the plains and mesas beyond, the moonlight turning the barren terrain into a spectral sculpture of shadow and silver. Yet hidden amongst the lifeless sands and wind-blasted rock were pockets of grazeland and grass valleys—where, Napier pointed out, had been some of the small spreads gobbled up by Triad Ranch.

That was about all Napier seemed prepared to say. All along he'd been acting oddly reticent, more than Jessie would have expected even from the usually taciturn cowboy. And whenever she tried discussing the Triad, or Folgeron, or the headband, or who Napier was and what he was up to, Napier promptly shoved her off the subject. He'd respond with something innocuous like, "Yeah, Folgeron's a smart dude. He reminds me of a rancher I used to know once o'er Laramie way, who . . ." And he'd ramble on about nothing to do with anything.

Riding on, they wended between tumbled rock masses, across minor arroyos, through shoulder-high brush. The Triad pursuers were shaken off now, left far back and lost in the labyrinthine badlands. Napier chose a canyon apparently no different from fifty others, and they followed the crooked V of its bottom for a half mile or so to its far end, which was bottlenecked by a dense copse of lodgepole pine and pignut saplings. Beyond, almost impossible to see for the trees, the canyon mouth widened into mesa country. Just before the trees lay a small, oval-shaped clearing, more akin to a wide patch cupped within the canyon. Along one side was a sort of cave-hut made by roofing a natural crevasse with flat slabs of shale and walling it in with gnarled logs lashed together with iron-tough wrappings of shrunken rawhide.

"It's an old line cabin," Napier said, as they reined in. "Belonged to the H-Bar-H, till Triad bought out the spread. From here we'll make a large circle and come in on Halfway Inn from the west, but first the horses need a rest and so do we. I reckon for the moment this's as safe a spot as any."

"Probably, but let's not take a long break."

"Long break, short break, there's things to be done."

Dismounting, Napier was peculiarly gallant, offering his hand to Jessie. She took it, his grip feeling firm yet gentle. Something stirred in her at the contact, and she held his hand tightly as she stepped from her saddle, then withdrew with a little laugh.

While Napier led their horses off into the trees and picketed them, Jessie warily checked out the cabin. Enough moonlight filtered in through the open doorway and front window for her to see a rough board table, a rusted potbelly iron stove, a couple of slab chairs and a double bunk against the rear wall. Napier returned with foodstuffs he'd been packing in his saddlebags, then made a second trip to gather firewood, careful to pick dry scraps that would burn with little smoke. There was a chill to the night air, and a few minutes of warmth, coupled with a hot meal, were worth the slight risk of detection.

After eating, Napier brought out the piece of hide he'd sliced off the steer and, with his hunting knife, began shaving off the hairs around the brand. Jessie regarded him, tight-lipped, unquestioning, until he held the hide against the stove's fire to see through it.

"Okay, Dutch, spill," she demanded testily. "I'm utterly confused, and I'd admire hearing right now what's going on and what's your part in it."

Napier stretched, sighed. "Someone's done a hasty job of branding, I'd judge, using too hot an iron that's burned through at one point. What intrigues me more is what the brand conceals. Have a look."

Taking the strip of hide from his outstretched hand, Jessie turned it this way and that, then extended it to the stove light the way he had done. A close scrutiny revealed that the brand did not read the same on both sides of the hide. On the outer side the brand read Triad. "It's been burned on top of another brand," she observed. "I can't quite tell what the other brand is, though. Is it yours?"

"Nope. I don't own a cow. Don't own much of anything 'cept my horse and the few personals it carries. A man with property is a man tied down. The last time I got tied down was by a New Mexico posse, and it didn't feel so good." He laughed as though jesting, then shook his head. "No, I figure it's the Block A brand out of Duck Valley, Idaho, reworked by rustlers."

"Is this what you came here to discover?"

"Just followed a hunch is all. I think Ki hit 'pon the same notion, back when we were overlooking the ranch and he said, 'Mighty handy.'" Napier tossed a chunk of wood into the firebox and watched it ignite, flaming up. Light glinted on the high spots of his eyes as he studied Jessie, sweeping her from head to foot. When he spoke again, his tone was restrained and guarded. "Remember, I pointed out how the ranch is partly in Oregon, partly in Idaho, with another cluster of buildings in Nevada. What a great layout for owlhoots with a price on their heads. Two states and a territory, each a separate jurisdiction. A fugitive on the run just has to cross the ranch yard from one jurisdiction to another, and he can thumb his nose at the law."

"Thinking of joining the Triad?"

"Why?"

"Dutch, you're the most exasperating man I've met in a month of Sundays," Jessie complained, returning the hide. "You've got a lot of names, and your talk of New Mexican posses makes me wonder if maybe some of your names aren't on wanted posters."

He smiled a little bitterly, a little longingly, and moved toward her. "I get into enough trouble just trying to avoid it without going on the dodge. I hate fighting,'specially gunfighting. But it seems there's no way I can quit if I want to stay living. Sometimes I wonder if it's worth the trouble."

"Don't talk like that," Jessie said. Something prompted her to meet his gaze—something she sensed rather than reasoned, something in his presence, in his deep eyes as they took their slow, bold fill of her. "You've done plenty of good here. You saved me and Ki from the Revengers. You've saved our lives from Blackjack Queeg, got Ki into the ranch and got us away. You've done more than anybody else in this godforsaken Devil's Playground." She placed a hand on his arm. "Would you like a job at my Circle Star?" When he failed to answer, she prodded him. "I mean as a cowpuncher, not a gunfighter. That's what you want, isn't it, Dutch?"

Napier averted his eyes. Jessie waited, breathless, drawn by the strong animal magnetism of him. It was nearly a suffocating force. When he looked at her again, it was pensively, as if her point were moot. "That's not in the cards for me, Jessie. Trouble dogs me wherever I go. It's something I can't get away from. I'd just bring trouble to Circle Star." Close now, he gripped her gently by the shoulders. "I'll be drifting on shortly."

"So you're just a saddle tramp."

Jessie saw the throbbing in the big blue vein that ran along Napier's temple and disappeared into his hairline. Then, without warning, his mouth trapped hers in a rough kiss. He held her hard and tight against him, then let her go, murmuring, "Do you make a habit of kissing saddle tramps?"

Trembling, she said, "I don't know why I let you do that."

"You were waiting for it. That's why, and you know it."

"That's not true," Jessie protested, eyes fever-bright. "If you try forcing me to kiss you again, I'll scream."

"Go ahead."

"Eek," she whispered.

Napier laughed and reached for her, his mouth coming down on hers once more. Her lips melted against his. Her arms slid around his neck. The hard buckle of his gunbelt pressed into the soft flesh of her waist. She couldn't get her breath, but she didn't care. She was caught up in an electric frenzy that seared a fiery path along her nerves. They kissed again, and again, lingeringly . . .

Then his hand slid down the front of her shirt. She felt his fingers cup one breast, his thumb and forefinger rolling her nipple, tweaking it into hardness. She stiffened once, then felt watery as, moaning into his kissing mouth, she felt his other hand begin kneading her other breast. She made no further effort to resist his fingers, urging him on wordlessly instead.

Almost before she was fully aware of it, Napier was undressing her. She helped by undressing him, garment for garment, until most of their clothing was piled up around their feet.

He stepped back then to admire her. "You're pretty."

She colored. "Dammit, you've made me blush!"

He grinned. "Well, I ain't about to lie and say you're ugly. Would you be so kind as to strip those drawers off'n that luscious fanny of yours, ma'am?"

"May I suggest the same, sir?" she countered teasingly, untying the drawstring and seductively easing her gauze-thin pantaloons down her legs. Hungrily she watched Napier removing the bottoms of his striped balbriggan underwear, letting her eyes roam over his broad, solidly planted figure.

"You're pretty," she told him.

His smile widened. "Aw, shucks, you'll make me blush," he said unblushingly, reaching for her, sending them both toppling to the cabin floor.

They wallowed there on the clothes and hard-packed dirt, stretching lengthwise, Jessie pressing against him. His arm was long. His hand was at the very base of her bottom, stroking, causing her cheeks to clench responsively. He tugged her closer, moving sideways a little more. Jessie moaned when she felt the touch of his fingers on the soft folds of her most

106

intimate parts. She squirmed, her moan becoming a sigh.

Again Napier shifted, his fingers moving deeper, yet only caressing with their tips. It was exquisite torture, and Jessie trembled under the inner glow of myriad tendrils of sensual pleasure. Those gentle fingers continued fondling her sensitive loins from behind, his forearm rubbing against her bottom. She noticed that her hips were writhing of their own volition, and now, increasingly, her moistening crevice was actually aching with impatience.

She slipped her mouth away from his and opened her eyes. "I want you," she whispered huskily in his ear. "I want you in me." Her admission touched off new sensations in her, and she writhed, her hand clutching at his muscular hip.

His hand slid from her parting inner thighs as he moved his lower torso inward to her, and his head began moving away, upward. She felt the hard length of his erection glide down to take the place of his hand, and she gasped, feeling it press against her anxious loins.

"Climb on top," he suggested. "You'll find it easier."

"And cleaner." She pivoted up, squatting over him, astride him, knees on the floor on either side of him.

"Put me in," he said in a quiet voice.

"Like this?" She gazed down at him with eyes filmed with passion, her hand centering his stabbing girth as she slowly impaled herself, contracting her strong inner thighs, her muscular action clamping her moist passage tightly around his shaft. "Ahh," she purred. "You're so huge!"

"You'll make me small," he told her, "all too soon."

"Hm!" she said wonderingly, squeezing tentatively.

He groaned. "Don't *do* that! Christ, you'll have me over and done with like a boy!" He let out a long breath as she relaxed.

"Think I can do that?"

"Might be fun to try sometime. Some other time."

"Not now? What now, then?"

"This," Napier said, and Jessie panted delightedly and half convulsed as he thrust his hips off the floor, ramming up into her.

Splaying her kneeling legs, she squirmed downward in response until she contained all of his rigid, lust-hardened length within her. Slowly at first, then with increasing fierceness, she began sliding up and down. This was a posture much to her liking, allowing her to be the dominant partner for a change, freeing her to control the pace and stimulation. Her head sagged, then tautened again in arousal, a vein standing out at the side of her throat with the fury of her pumping exertion. Her mouth opened and closed in mute testimony to the exquisite sensations plundering her loins, her long hair swaying and brushing down over her shoulders and across his chest.

Napier grasped her jiggling breasts, toying harshly with them until hoarse moans were drawn from her slackened lips. She bent for a brief moment with a whisper of a kiss, then arched up and back as she plunged deeper, faster, reaching behind to caress Napier's scrotum, massaging with delicately stroking fingernails. The backward angle made her body toss precariously on his hips, her thighs descending with building force, only to reverse at the last instant and draw up again on his penetrating manhood.

Napier, tensing upward, felt the gripping of her sheath tearing at his entrails. "God, Jessie, you're like a vise," he panted.

Her passage kept gripping, gripping, as she crooned above him, her mouth open, her eyes wide and sightless. The gripping grew unbearable until, shuddering, he erupted violently with a massive climax. Jessie's loins worked and sucked as if his juices were some invigorating tonic, to be ravenously swallowed in her belly, as her face contorted and twisted in the throes of her own spasming orgasm.

Then, with the ebb of passion, Jessie crouched limp and satiated over Napier. Slowly, sighing contentedly, she eased off his flaccid body and lay down alongside him, feeling drugged, unable to move. She wanted to say something but was at a loss for words. Instead, she silently nestled against him while she sank into a delightful lethargy.

"Just for a second," she murmured. "Then we'll get dressed . . ."

The next thing she knew, groggily, she was being disturbed from a deep, dreamless sleep by Napier easing from beside her. "Relax," he whispered sooth-ingly, slipping on his clothes. "I need to water the grass is all. And I ought to see that nobody's snooping on our backtrail."

Lulled, Jessie drifted off again . . . For exactly how long, she wasn't sure, but it couldn't have been more than a few minutes. Something, then, some intuition or subconscious instinct, aroused her. "Dutch?" she called out.

Silence.

"Dutch!" She sat upright, still woozy with sleep.

No answer, no sign of the man.

Padding to the doorway, Jessie peered out and about. She saw nothing, but now she caught the sound of faint galloping from the far end of the clearing, receding downtrail beyond the copse of trees. "I don't believe this!" she snapped, a twinge of self-consciousness stealing over her as she sprinted naked across the clearing and into the trees.

Where Napier had picketed their horses, only her pinto remained. Her saddle gear was still on the ground, where he had stacked it neatly beside his after stripping both mounts. His roan and gear were gone. The only thing he had left behind was a pair of wire clippers, which he had laid conspicuously on top of her gear.

Running through to the other side of the copse, Jessie stared hard down the trail in the direction she had heard the hoofbeats. She expected to catch sight of Napier—if at all—on the lope across the mesa land beyond the canyon. Instead, like an opti-cal illusion, he appeared in another direction with a next-to-impassable gorge between them. Napier seemed to sense she had spotted him, for he reined, turning in his saddle, and waved to her.

"Goddamn you, Dutch Napier! Come back here!"

Of course Napier did nothing of the sort, riding away and out of sight around a curve of the country, leaving Jessie blistering the night air about men in general and a certian rakehell in particular. Yet, as she started back to the cabin for her clothes, there was a touch of admiration in her voice. It wasn't often a man bested Jessie, or diverted her from her intentions. Napier had, changing the subject and shutting her up in grand style. She had no regrets on that score. Trouble was, Napier had now embarked upon an expedition of his own and left no forwarding address.

It wasn't long before Jessie was remounted and heading out. Initially her urge had been to ride back around to the Triad ranchstead and try to locate Ki, who might well be in need of help there. But she thought better of it. The Triad range would be a hornet's nest, no doubt, with riders out in force. Not only would it be extremely dangerous for her to return, but what if Ki had gone into the ranch and came out again and was already on his way to a rendezvous at Halfway Inn? Jessie decided to hew to the line they'd agreed upon.

Crossing the mesa, she entered a maze of twisting canyons and crooked ridges, hoping her sense of direction would not fail her, scouting steadily for sign that would lead her to the remote roadhouse. Gradually the peaks grew smaller, more rounded, the clefts shallower and dotted with mesquite and cactus. Pretty soon she traversed a stretch of scalloped rangeland, and came up against the Triad fenceline, its many strands of barbed wire glinting in the moonlight.

Taking the wire cutters Napier had left—and reminding herself to thank him for them after she killed him—Jessie snipped a strand. She cut another strand and another, pausing between each for a searching look around, but nothing stirred. Finally the last strand was severed, and she forced her mount through the opening.

From here she believed she could locate the trail that went past Halfway Inn. Twice she followed false sign and had to backtrack, the wasted effort frustrating her, making her edgy. With time and perseverance, she forged through roughs of brush, rock and piñon and eventually reached the trail— or what she presumed was the right trail, figuring where it should run in relation to the land. The trail unwound like a drunken ribbon between ridges and gullies and the pervasive jagged hills, seeming vaguely familiar to her . . . but so, she had to admit, would just about any trail through this infernal wilderness. The pinto quickened its pace as if sensing the end of the journey.

There was a suspicious grayness, the false dawn, by the time Jessie glimpsed Halfway Inn looming ahead. Lamplight glowed from the windows of the main tavern downstairs, a hopeful sign to her as she entered the yard. She went first to the stable to tend to her pinto and look for Ki's sorrel. But the

112

only horse she found was a piebald mare, still warm from a recent workout. Thinking perhaps Ki might have had to switch mounts to get here, she slapped her own horse into a stall with water and feed and hurried across to the inn.

"Ki!" she called, seeing a lone figure in the tavern. "Ki!"

Then Jessie was staring in surprise, for it was a young woman—a corn-silk blonde, wearing a black silk shirt and a forked leather skirt, a woman who'd been sitting at one of the tables, her head resting upon her folded arms, sleeping. Jessie's wild entry had brought her awake, and she glanced up with wide eyes and a frightened intake of breath.

Jessie, taken aback, blurted, "Where's Ki?"

"M-Miss Starbuck? Jessica Starbuck?"

Nodding, smiling to calm the woman's fears, Jessie said, "I'm sorry I startled you. I was looking for Ki, a friend of mine."

"Ah, yes, Ki. The brave man who came to my rescue."

"Why, that must mean your name is Laverna."

"Yes, Laverna Pegaso." Hesitantly, Laverna gave a brief account of Ki's entry into her bedroom and the incident at the gate, editing out some of their goings-on in between. "He told me to meet him here," she concluded. "I got to the fence and found the gate open. All night I've ridden off-trail, keeping concealed, constantly watchful, and only arrived a short while ago, very tired."

Jessie had spied the headband which Laverna still wore. "Ki give you the headband?"

"Also a fat letter," Laverna replied, indicating the front of her shirt. "I'm to keep them until he's able to join me. Alas, I fear he was captured after enabling me to escape."

"If he hasn't gotten here by now, I fear you're right," Jessie said agitatedly. "I fear Ki's in bad trouble!"

★

Chapter 10

Ki was indeed in bad trouble. Bad as death.

A voice rose from the dark cloud of his unconsciousness. "More water on him, Blackjack! He's
waking up."

Frigid wetness splashed against him, shocking
him into reality. Now, more clearly, but still hidden
in the gauze wool of pain and dizziness, Ki could
hear another voice say, "There, that should do it.
He's beginning to move."

Gradually the mists faded, though Ki could still
not make sense of what was happening around him.
His first true thought was that he was drowning in a
sea of agony. Then slowly he realized he was merely
dripping wet, stripped to the waist and shivering
from the dousing. He tried to change his position,
and it was then that the second realization struck
him—that he was hanging from a crude, homemade
strappado. The strappado was a quaintly prehistoric
forerunner of the rack, a simple yet brutal torture of
hoisting a victim into the air by metal wrist bracelets. Strung upright, one's weight was suspended by

the arms, and chains attached to the shackles ran up and over a thick crossbeam, to be raised or lowered at will. Sudden jerkings and wrenchings soon ripped muscles, dislocated sockets, broke bones.

Dangling, Ki sucked in air to clear his head, then gazed around. Judging by the lamplit stone walls and foul air, he was in a basement or root cellar of the ranchstead, doubtlessly dragged down here unconscious after the fight. His shirt and vest were dumped in the corner next to the thick plank door. A few feet in front of him were the scowling countenances of Enoch Hyde and Blackjack Queeg.

"Lucky for you I got to the gate at the last minute," Hyde growled at Ki. "Elsewise you'd be dead. You ain't, not yet. You're gonna live long enough to talk, to tell me what fetched you here."

Ki managed a foggy, no-brains-at-all grin. "Why, you did, Mr. Folgeron. Don't you recollect the invite you sent Miss Starbuck?"

Hyde looked jolted, and puzzled.

"She changed her mind, y'see," Ki continued, to confound the lawyer further. "The more she got to thinking about it, the more she reckoned that Mexican expedition of yours might have its points. Sorry about roughing up your crew, but when we tried visitin' respectable-like, we nigh got ourselves executed."

Blackjack Queeg giggled at that, and put on a little show, very brief. Stepping to the wall behind the strappado, he took down a coiled bullwhip, waggled his jaw, and rolled his eyes a couple of times.

"Stop it!" roared Hyde. Queeg had already stopped,

holding the whip snaked out behind him. Hyde, turning back to Ki, said, "You're here on behalf of Miss Starbuck, eh? So I imagine that makes you Ki, that meddlesome flunky she's known to keep around. Well, for your information, I'm not Winthrop Folgeron. I'm his attorney, Enoch Hyde. Folgeron has passed away."

"Y'don't say! And how perchance did he die?"

In a low, ominous voice, Hyde said, "I killed him."

"Yes," Ki said, as if believing it, although he suspected Laverna had told the truth and Hyde was simply trying to intimidate him. "Did you brace Folgeron man to man? Or did you tell him a dirty joke and kill him whilst he laughed?"

Enoch Hyde spat and said, "You don't care much whether you live or die, do you? What you don't seem to've fathomed yet is that nobody can save you, nothing can stop me. I'm Winthrop Folgeron's sole heir and can prove it by a will that will stand in any court. I'm master of Triad Ranch, and I want to know what you're doing, breaking in here."

When Ki ignored him scornfully, as he would a child, Blackjack Queeg snarled, "Answer him." And, at a nod from Hyde, Queeg snapped out the whip.

The pain was excruciating as the rawhide coiled around Ki's bare torso. He writhed in his dangling position, heaving in an arc. He had to stall, to feed Hyde enough to delay the inevitable, and pray . . .

"Okay, okay," Ki said through gritting teeth. "The way we figured it, Folgeron had asked Miss Starbuck to come here. When he died, which must have been recently, you knew she was en route. You didn't want

117

us snooping about the ranch, so you schemed to meet her in Beyond and pass yourself off as Folgeron. And since she'd likely grow suspicious if you claimed her visit was all a mistake, you spun a windy about mounting an expedition to Mexico."

"Apparently you two suspected me anyway. How come?"

"A button. I picked one up at Halfway Inn, tore it off an hombre who snatched a woman away from there in the darkness," Ki replied, careful not to mention her name or that she had written a message for help. "When you showed up in Beyond, Miss Starbuck noticed you had a button missing from your coat."

Hyde glanced at his sleeve, then back at Ki, glaring. "Well, bucko, the woman is missing. You succeeded in getting Laverna away from here."

Gratified to hear she had made her escape, Ki smiled tightly, his mouth just crimping at the lower corners.

"And she must have the headband," Hyde went on, his voice loaded with meaning. "You must've snuck into my bedroom, taken it before you got out of the house. You passed it to her, didn't you? Where is she? Where'd she go with it?"

"Don't know what you're talking about."

"You think I can't break you?" Hyde snarled, and then nodded.

Again Queeg struck Ki with the whip, leaving another scarlet streak on his bare flesh. Ki fought the chains that held him, throwing his weight against them, trying to dodge the flaying strokes.

But Queeg was a master of his craft, and he never missed.

"Tell me, boy! Tell me while you can!"

Hyde's voice blurred as Queeg hit Ki again and again. A scream echoed in the room, and only when it had died did Ki realize it was his own. He had to have a respite. He had to get Queeg to stop or he'd never find a way out of this horror. With a groan, he let his head fall forward in feigned unconsciousness, allowing his muscles to hang slack and unresponsive. Queeg applied the lash three more times, but somehow Ki managed to stifle his screams and keep his body inert. After a minute he heard the whip fall to the floor.

Hyde was furious. "You went too far, you idiot! Wake him up!"

"You'll have to wait."

"I can't wait! I've got to get that band back—"

Interrupting him was the sound of boots thumping down a flight of stairs just outside, then a hard-knuckled rapping on the door. Remaining limp, Ki heard Blackjack Queeg open the door and step outside, where he spoke briefly with someone in grumbling mutters, too low to discern. Queeg called for Hyde to step out, and the muffled conversation continued. Ki listened intently, to no avail, the sweat trickling down his body, stinging the raw welts. Then Hyde's voice became clearer as he turned back to the room—evidently to check on Ki and reach for the door latch—and Ki heard him saying, " . . . learn different from the Dutchman, but I still think it's mostly that female who's responsible

119

for him coming here. Let him hang for now."

The door slammed shut with a hollow thud.

Ki was alone. He raised his head, glancing around and wondering how long he had until Hyde or Queeg returned. Bracing his feet against the stone wall, he pulled himself up to clutch the chains above his shackles. His fingers were slippery, but he held on. Taking a deep breath, he started climbing hand over hand as fast as he could. He could feel the muscles of his shoulders and arms straining to the breaking point, but he kept shinnying upward.

Just as he reached the thick crossbeam, he caught the sound of approaching footsteps again. Desperately he hooked his leg over the beam and hauled himself into a straddling position, then worked furiously to free himself from the shackles. There were mere split seconds before whoever was coming opened the door, saw him and whipped him back into submission.

The shackles were as ancient as their torture, fastened by simple link pins. The door creaked open, then Blackjack Queeg's shadow stretched across the stone floor. In the same instant, Ki drew the pins out and released the bracelets. One pin fell, and Queeg glanced up, seeing Ki. Cursing, he stooped for the bullwhip on the floor. Snaking it back, his features contorted with fury.

Ki gathered the heavy iron chain as fast as he could and swung it in a loop. The open shackle slammed into Queeg's temple, and howling, he crashed back against the door, then crumpled to the floor. Ki sprang at him, landing full force on his chest. Queeg groaned, seeming to deflate, but Ki didn't pause to see what damage he'd done, snagging his shirt and vest as he raced out the door, and tossing them on while climbing the steps, two at a time.

At the top of the stairs, he realized he was back in the large pantry that led to the kitchen, dining room, library and the rest of the main ranch house. It also led outside. He headed for the outer door, the one he had picked unlocked hours before, and was surprised to find it wide open now. Stopping flat against the doorjamb, he peered around the corner.

Directly outside was parked a farm wagon and team. Two crewmen were sitting in the wagon box, the bed behind them packed with boxes, sacks and barrels of foodstuffs. Their chore was to unload the supplies into the pantry, Ki guessed, but there was a commotion going on in the direction of the main gate, and the men were taking advantage of it to loaf. One had a pint of whiskey and was offering it to the other man slouched beside him. The second man put out his hand to take it, then hesitated and glanced about uneasily as if sensing something was wrong.

Ki drew back, willing himself invisible.

The first man wiped the lip of the bottle and thrust it out again, and this time, shrugging, the second man accepted it. He raised it to his lips for a hefty swig, while the first man went to stroking his chin. The first was stroking and nodding approvingly when there came a feathery whisper from the doorway, and a needle-tipped dagger suddenly pinned his hand to his throat.

The drinking man choked, dropping the bottle. "Wha—" he began, as his buddy rolled off the wagon seat. He abruptly shuddered, gurgling, puzzled about the knife blade that had slashed clear through his throat; he actually had time to finger the bloodied dagger before crumpling alongside the first man, both men now mutually dead.

Ki felt no compunction about killing them. Back in early evening, when he and Jessie had bumped into Blackjack Queeg and his boys, that rabid *segundo* had recognized Jessie by name. So he must've known that his boss wanted her out of the way, that Enoch Hyde didn't care whether she went to Mexico or died on the spot, just so long as she and anyone with her left the Devil's Playground pronto. It meant Queeg and his boys were a killer crew, privy to whatever Hyde was up to. And to Ki, that meant kill or be killed.

At this point, his hope was that once past the wagon, he could sneak over the wall, grab his horse and dust out before any alarm could be raised. The fight and Queeg's whipping had left him battered, bloodied and sore all over, muscles cramping, drained of energy. It had been a punishing struggle just to force himself this far.

However, although the light was poor and the angle bad, Ki could make out the action at the front gate. A squad of Triad riders was filing through with a prisoner on horseback: Dutch Napier. Ki now understood the interruption in the cellar—a crewman had rushed to report Napier's capture, and Hyde's last words had been in regard to that.

Yet Hyde had referred to a "female," which Ki had assumed was Laverna. Now he feared Hyde had meant Jessie. What had happened to her? Where was she? Wounded ? Dead?

Napier alone knew, and he was caught. Or . . . ?

Leaping to the wagon box, Ki flung out the bodies and gave the reins a whiplike crack. Instantly the team bolted, yanking the wagon forward and pitching Ki backward. He straightened, fighting for balance as he sent the wagon slewing around the patio and tearing for the main gate. It was a frantic, suicidal effort to rescue Napier—or at least allow him to save himself. And it was guaranteed to fail.

For a second, the riders and bystanders were shocked immobile. But facing a runaway team and wagon bearing down on them, they swiftly recovered and began triggering guns to halt the charge. Gust after gust of hot lead rent the air. Ki ducked low, hurrawing the team on faster. A bullet, ricocheting off a metal seat bracket, angled up through the front panel and slashed a bloody furrow along the broad rump of one of the horses. The piercing whinnies of first one, then both, lunging horses and the raucous clatter of the wagon added to the noisy bedlam. The frenzied animals plunged headlong into the midst of the riders, a flying wedge plowing through to the gateway, Ki wrestling a set of taut reins that wrenched and jerked like angry snakes in his hands.

It seemed to him that perhaps, just maybe, he might make it. He gestured to Napier—then Napier vanished, consumed in the welter of men and horse-flesh. Before Ki could catch sight of him again, the team whirled completely about, ramming into each other, and careening against the gate. The wild swerve had tilted the wagon dangerously, and Ki fought to balance it with his weight. He felt the wagon lean beyond its center of gravity, the cargo tumbling over and spilling out.

"Shit!" he yelled, releasing the reins and diving off. The wagon broadsided the stone-walled portal and tipped over, just as he threw himself free. He struck, tumbling outside the entrance across gravel and gritty earth, hearing the shrill cries of the team wrenching against their harnesses, the snapping breakage of wooden slats and staves, the crunching smash of wagon boards and wheel spokes entangling in the iron bars of the gate.

Dark, raging confusion boiled all around as, scrambling to his feet, Ki sprinted for the stable where he'd tethered his horse. Lead searched after him, but the busted wagon and cargo had temporarily barricaded the gateway, and the Triad crewmen were too routed to shoot effectively, their bullets zinging off-target, some close, some wild. He heard galloping hoofbeats descending on him, and pivoted, aiming to launch a *shuriken* or two at the rider.

"No! It's me! Henk Willem Adrian—"

"Never mind the rest of it!" Ki shouted back, glimpsing Napier astride the roan. "Let's get my horse and get out of here!"

He dived into the stable, knowing they had scant time before the crewmen regrouped and came storming after them from every angle. They badly needed a diversion. As he tightened the cinch on his sorrel, Ki glanced wildly about, but all he could spot were the other horses, a couple of saddle blankets, a lengthy piece of rope and a kerosene lantern hanging on a peg. On impulse, he took down the lantern, finding that it sloshed, full. Around him, the stabled horses were snorting restively, prancing skittishly as savage rifle fire peppered the walls, some of the heavier caliber bullets drilling through.

He yelled to Napier, "Free the horses!"

"What'n hell?"

"Quick! Set 'em loose!"

Hastily Napier wheeled his roan along the stable row, while Ki knotted one end of the rope around a corner of a blanket, then emptied the lantern's reservoir of kerosene over the blanket. With reins and rope in hand, he climbed asaddle his sorrel, struck a match, and cast Napier a grin.

"Ready?"

"Hours ago! Che-rist!"

Ki tossed the match on the blanket. Its kerosene-soaked fabric ignited with a high-flaming burst. His sorrel took one look and went berserk.

And so did every other horse in the stable.

"Hiiyaa!" Ki shouted, heeling his mount into a dead-heat gallop. It bucked and winged to get rid of the fire on its tail, which panicked the other horses all that much more. "Hiiyaa!"

The horses stampeded crazily, whinnying and pawing and crashing out of the stable in hysterical frenzy. They collided pell-mell with a host of

125

crewmen who were just launching an assault on the stable. Pistols roared, men scrambled and the horses ran amok. Behind all the hullabaloo rode Napier and Ki, whose frantic mount was still scrambling to escape the flapping, crackling terror that insistently chased it.

They veered down among the huts toward the fields. Napier took the lead, knowing how best to go, hunching low to avoid being hit by some of the cooler-headed gunmen firing at them. Ki followed close, but to hell with staying down; his concern was staying in the saddle and heading his sorrel in the right direction. Following third was a lengthening trail of fire. And farther back, going nowhere, were the horses milling and romping insanely in among the buildings, plus the gunmen, who were busily dodging the horses, not knowing where to turn but figuring moving to keep from being trampled beat standing still.

The blanket, with its blaze whipped and fanned to a livid fury, kindled some of the old, weather-dried plank boards of the shanties. Ki, glancing over his shoulder, saw that their backtrail was burning and spreading like a smoldering wake. And yonder near the ranchstead, ribbons of smoke were squirreling upward from the eaves of the stable, the hay and dry timber inside it having ignited on Ki's way out.

"Ride! Ride!" Ki called urgently.

They flogged on with tuckering horses to the fields, not worrying about line riders, who would surely have been drawn to the fires. The stable and surrounding structures were geysering flames and mushrooming clouds of smoke. A night breeze was blowing the smoke, sparks and cinders back toward the ranchstead, and while Ki couldn't be sure, it appeared to him that the fire had spread over the wall. Reaching the fields, he let go of the rope, reckoning it was the wrong season for crops to burn and that the blanket had done enough of a job. His notion had been to cause a distraction; burning the shacks and torching the ranch house were extras he was grateful for, but unplanned— nothing this spectacular could've been. Three for the price of one, at the cost of a permanently paranoid horse. Not bad.

When they reached the slope at the eastern edge of the valley, they ascended to the rimrocks and reined in for a breather. Behind, the stable and numerous huts were collapsing in showers of flame, and inside the ranchstead wall, buildings were ablaze so fiercely, the very air seemed to be burning.

Ki turned to Napier. "All right, what're you doing here?"

"Why, rescuing you." When he saw the coldly furious astonishment on Ki's face, Napier quickly argued, "I agreed to raise a fuss so you could sneak in the ranch, but I never promised not to come myself."

"Uh-huh. To save me. It had nothing to do with making sure you got the headband and maybe Laverna," Ki retorted caustically. "Well, you'll be glad to hear that she's out of there, and she has the band. Now, where's Jessie?"

"Safe," Napier said with a little shrug. "After we raised our fuss and got away, I thought it best to, ah, ditch her where she'd be safe. She's very brave, but there wasn't any reason why she should share the risks any further."

Ki had to chuckle. "I'll bet Jessie won't thank you for your concern. Likely she's gone to Halfway Inn. I sent Laverna there, too."

They made a beeline straight for the Triad fence line, and found the entry gate there still unlocked. And no riders were nearby to challenge their exit.

★

Chapter 11

Jessie was not at Halfway Inn.

It was midmorning when Ki and Dutch Napier arrived. Tethering their horses at the water trough and entering the inn, they found Laverna Pegaso alone in the barroom's grubby kitchen, cooking an omelette on a three-burner wood stove. A moment was spent acknowledging one another, a brief reunion with surprise and relief and an introduction tossed in. Then Laverna put on coffee and began mixing up an extra big bowl of her self-proclaimed specialty—eggs, onions, green peppers and chopped ham, to make omelettes for the men.

She gave Ki a long, fretful look. "How did it go?"

Ki didn't reply; his appearance was answer enough.

"It went okay," Napier responded, as if to shrug it off. "A little snarling and baring of teeth."

"Watch out for those Triad teeth," Laverna said. "They don't only bare. They can make a mighty mean bite." She dropped an egg in the coffee and tended the omelettes. "Oh, Jessie Starbuck told me to tell you,

129

if y'all showed up, to stay put till she got back."

"She did? She was here? Where'd Jessie go?"

"I don't know, Ki. We talked some, read Winthrop's letter you gave me, then she took his headband and lit out. She didn't say to where, only about this having to stop once'n for all."

Napier grimaced. "Now *she's* got the band."

"Cheer up, I've still got the letter," Laverna said, and after they were seated at a table, the omelettes before them, she removed the envelope from her blouse. "I'm to give this back to you, Ki. Jessie told me she's going to hand Dutch something else, something personal, too, with wire clippers."

Ki laughed, catching Napier's pained expression. "I'll read it aloud." He opened the envelope and shook out the flimsy sheets of the letter, instantly recognizing the same handwriting as on the note passed to Jessie by the hotel clerk. " 'This is the testament of one who realizes late in his years that his life has been misspent,' " Ki began. " 'My early life is unimportant, other than to confess my career as a photographer, a collector of imagery, instilled in me an avarice which I've since come to deplore. To those who have suffered by my greed, I make this apology and this attempt at restitution.' "

"A good man," Laverna sniffed, dabbing a tear. "Winthrop was a good man at heart."

Ki nodded, dry-eyed. " 'In my middle years, I founded Triad Ranch to house my photography, my art and Indian collections. The legalities were handled by Enoch Hyde, a lawyer by trade and rogue by nature. Soon I regarded Triad like another

130

collection, to be expanded and hoarded. With Enoch Hyde's faculty for finding loopholes, I ousted a number of land holders whose names I've appended to this—' "

"The Revengers!" Napier exclaimed.

" 'My will,' " Ki continued, " 'prepared many years ago, made Enoch Hyde my sole heir and is in his possession. After my change of heart, I informed him I planned to restore the lands to those I'd robbed, even though the robbery was technically legal. He scoffed, grew belligerent. I then secretly prepared a new will, in which the lands revert to their rightful holders, my Indian collection goes to the Department of the Interior, and the balance of my estate to Laverna Pegaso—' "

Laverna began crying softly, and Ki hastily resumed his reading. " 'Of late I've realized that my life is in danger. I made the mistake of telling Enoch Hyde of my new will, and I've reason to believe he has been scheming against me with my foreman, a man Hyde insisted I hire, Blandon Queeg.' "

"Blackjack Queeg," Napier growled, interrupting again. "Yessir, Winthrop Folgeron signed his own death warrant when he let Hyde know of his intentions. Queeg is a notorious killer who once headed a rustling gang in Idaho. No doubt Folgeron wasn't too keen about the ranching end of things, and Hyde duped him into hiring Queeg quite easily. Then Queeg, working secretly for Hyde, saw fit to organize another rustling combine, brung in his own owlhoot crew, and began using Triad's bought-out brands to market stolen cattle."

"And now Folgeron's death has brought matters to a climax," Ki observed, then returned to reading: " 'I have advised the Department of the Interior of my situation. I have also requested the aid of Miss Jessica Starbuck, who has an impeccable reputation for integrity, and powerful resources to back her. As added precaution, I prepared this document, which I left in my library, and I arranged to have a note delivered to Miss Starbuck in Beyond. In the event of my death, I hereby commission Miss Starbuck to see that my last will is carried out, and that my murderers are brought to justice. Should Miss Starbuck refuse payment for her services, I hereby bequeath her any two art works from my library.' " The vision of Jessie choosing a couple of those pictures set Ki to laughing again. Sobering, he finished the letter: " 'Among my Indian artifacts is a rare Tukudeka ceremonial headband. For safety, I have concealed my last will under a specially sewn sweat lining in the headband.' "

Dutch Napier spread his hands. "There. Now you understand why I'm after the headband, and why I'm piss—er, upset to learn it's gone."

"I'm beginning to understand plenty," Ki replied, folding the letter back into the envelope. "Enoch Hyde has had two worries—one to get rid of Jessie, the other to get rid of Folgeron's second will. But I bet it wasn't till last night that he realized he'd been packing that will inside the headband all along and never knew it. When the headband started interesting outsiders, Hyde saw the light. Now he'll be hotfooting it after us for sure."

132

"Hyde had another worry," Laverna said. "Me. He grew violently angry after Winthrop died, when I wouldn't marry him. I tried leaving the ranch, but he caught up with me here. It was while he was in the hall that I signaled you, Ki, seeing you in the yard, and failing that, I traced a message in the dust on the windowsill."

"But Hyde got suspicious," Ki guessed, "and dragged you from the room, clouting me down when I got in his way. I see his notion. He wanted his mitts on Folgeron's heir, and the marriage idea was so he'd be master of Triad even if the new will did show up. If he couldn't persuade you to marry him, he would've had to kill you. And that's still true, I reckon." Ki turned to Dutch Napier. "Well, chum? You're the one player who hasn't laid his cards out."

"I," Napier answered with a dramatic flourish, "am the Department of the Interior."

"All of it?" Laverna gasped.

"Oh, no, ma'am. There're several other agents besides myself. The information which Winthrop Folgeron sent the government was turned over to me. His Indian artifact collection is not only reputed to be museum quality, but to've been gathered somewhat questionably, like his ranch. My mission was to investigate his troubles, and insure his collection would go to the Department, as willed. But on the trail to Triad, I stopped here for directions, was sidetracked off to an abandoned homestead, and got waylaid by Queeg and his boys. Next I knowed, I awoke back here. Then the fracas started, and I thought better of sticking around for the finale."

Napier grinned ruefully at Laverna, drawling softly, "Please pardon this poor bungler who failed you in your moment of peril. Had I but knowed . . ."

Laverna colored.

Ki choked on his last bite of omelette. "Yes, well, now we all know where we stand," he said, getting up from the table. "Since we're waiting for Jessie, I think I'll go stable my horse."

"Good idea," Napier agreed, joining him. "I've got a roan that could use some grooming and a forkload of hay."

"While you're at it, Dutch," Laverna asked, "give my mare a big fork too, will you?"

"If he's up to it," Ki murmured on their way out.

From the trough, they led their mounts into the stable for tending, using a couple of old ratty brushes and combs Ki found amidst the clutter. Napier climbed to a loft with a pitchfork and ladled hay down into the mangers below, including some for Laverna's piebald mare. When he descended, he said, "I couldn't help noticin' up there, that in the empty stall at the far end is a mound of dirt, like a fresh-dug grave."

"It is. That's where I buried the dead proprietor for safekeeping," Ki answered, and related the finale of the fracas Napier had missed, concluding, "Thinking back on it, the proprietor got shot with his own gun. Hyde had lost his while fighting me, but there wasn't any sound of struggle after he ran downstairs. Meaning he didn't take the proprietor's gun away; the proprietor must've handed it over. Meaning the proprietor was in cahoots with Hyde."

Napier swore. "That explains how I got misdirected, and Queeg knew where to waylay me. Yeah, and how Hyde caught Laverna when she stopped here—"

"*Shhh!*" Ki admonished.

Out yonder, toward the front of the inn, came a faint creaking, like saddle leather, and a clicking noise like that made by the beat of horses' irons on stony ground. Ki crept to the stable doorway and peered cautiously outside, Napier at his elbow. Ahead, a horde of horsemen were trooping into the clearing, and there was no trouble identifying Enoch Hyde and Blackjack Queeg among the hardcase crew. Queeg in particular stood out; his bruised face was purple and puffed, and smeared with a yellow salve, half-melted and running in trickles down his seamed throat.

"Appears Enoch Hyde has caught up with us," Napier growled. "Appears we'll have to make a hot fight to defend a headband we ain't got."

The Triad riders were sitting their saddles in a tight knot, talking among themselves, and snatches of the talk floated over to the stable. The question seemed to be whether or not Halfway Inn was deserted as it seemed, a waste of time to search; most opined it was worthwhile stopping, if only to take a piss.

"If we can get back inside the inn, we'll make it a tough job for Hyde no matter the odds," Napier said, rising. "C'mon. Let's grab the saddle carbines here—you *can* shoot, can't you?—and run for the rear door."

"Wait," Ki countered. "We can fort up in the inn with the doors barred and the windows shuttered, okay, but what about that outside staircase to the second-floor fire door? We've got to stop Hyde from sending men up there and catching us inside from upstairs. Maybe if we tossed a couple of loops . . ."

"Y'mean like cow-roping? Consider yourself good, do you?"

"I've twirled a lasso once or twice. And as for shooting, hell, I've been known to fire a gun three times in a row, and that's a fact."

"Wonderful," Napier groaned.

Slipping back into the stable for their horses, they heard Enoch Hyde proclaim, "It won't take more than ten minutes for us to have a look in every nook 'n' cranny of the place. I want to comb 'er fine, Blackjack."

Hurriedly they resaddled their horses, Ki spending a moment to snatch a coil of rope and a Winchester .44—40 from Laverna's saddle gear. Then, pausing at the stable door, they saw that now the Triad crew was dismounted, and Hyde was starting toward the inn, Queeg falling in a pace behind.

"A couple of you jiggers have a look in the barn," Blackjack Queeg ordered. "The rest of you tag along with me."

"Here goes nuthin'!" Napier snapped, and bending low to avoid the doorway, he and Ki launched their horses charging out of the stable.

"Goddamn it, it's them!" Hyde barked in startled rage, hopping to hook his stirrup. "Don't just stand there, kill 'em!"

136

Ki and Napier headed straight for the inn, gunshots snapping and whining after them as they swerved in alongside the building. Already they had uncoiled their lariats and tied them by one end to their saddlehorns, much as Napier had done when he bulldogged the steer to cut out its brand. Now, almost floundering as they veered past the staircase, they whipped lassos out and up to snag the protruding posts of the landing above, prodding their mounts on at full gallop.

The Triad gang, scrambling asaddle, was hastily spurring after, sending lead sizzling by their heads. Their ropes drew taut, the landing and staircase wobbling, beginning to splinter, but not yet managing to break. Cussing and kicking flanks, they urged their horses straining forward, while behind them, revolvers and rifles blasted away—in a suddenly erratic fashion, as crewmen were scattered by a salvo of covering gunfire blazing from a barroom window.

"Good ol' Laverna!" Napier yelled.

His voice was drowned out by ripping nails and cracking boards. The upper landing parted from the fire door, followed by the staircase peeling away from the side of the building, the whole rickety structure plummeting to the ground with a horrendous crash, dust and dirt erupting through the wreckage.

Consternation reigned among the Triad crew, most slowing, wheeling about. Those in front, such as Hyde and Queeg, were wreathed in plumes of grit, fighting plunging horses, bullets sailing off—high, low and wild.

The slackening allowed Ki and Napier a momentary reprieve. They dismounted at a run with carbines and extra ammo in hand, spanked their horses out of range, and sprinted to the rear stoop just as Laverna opened the door.

Covering their entrance with a blaze of pistol fire, Laverna slammed and barred the door behind them. Triad bullets shattered the window next to the door, and Napier, ducking reflexively, smashed out the rest of the glass with the butt of his carbine. "Christ, they're a right big bunch!"

At Ki's elbow, Laverna was reloading a well-abused Remington .44–40; her Bisley revolver was still holstered high on her left side. "I found the gun behind the bar counter," she told Ki, catching his curious glance. "The proprietor probably stowed it there for a backup. I also found some boxes of .44–40 cartridges, which won't fit my own piece."

"Some is better than none," Ki said, handing her the carbine he'd taken from her saddle gear. "Afraid?"

"Petrified. But I keep reminding myself, *they're* the ones outside. We're under cover of walls, and they don't know how many of us are in here."

"Guess that's so" Napier allowed, turning toward the front of the barroom. "You two stay here. I'll take the window by the entrance."

Glass fell from the front window, sending Napier running to head off the attack. Meanwhile, a number of Queeg's renegade crew came piling in at the rear window. This was neither the time nor place for martial arts; Ki chambered his saddle carbine and triggered out the broken window. So did Laverna, and she was a caution to see firing. Three stabs of flame leapt from her carbine, three sharp reports blending almost as one—and three stupefied men staggered from three separate angles, and fell.

Up at the entrance, soft-drawling Dutch Napier muttered epithets steadily as he worked both carbine and revolver. A half-breed gunman just outside the bullet-spattered panes let out a cry and clawed at his chest, spurting blood on his calfskin vest. Then he vanished, while the man next to him swore in pain as he crawled off, hit in the shoulder. The door and window framing rattled with the impact of Triad slugs. But the negligently daring Napier kept on firing right from the window, drilling slugs out across the clearing.

The house was completely surrounded, Ki knew. The outside staircase was down, but was there any other way the Triad crew could gain the upper floor? Leaving Laverna to cover the rear of the building, Ki headed up the stairs. He had a quick look around; from the window of the fire door, he saw swift scurrying movement at the edge of the clearing. He levered and again let fly with his carbine, hoping he'd cause them to believe that the upstairs had defenders, too.

He brought down one man. Two others stumbled over him, and Laverna's carbine below, kicking up dust dangerously near them, sent them in wild rout. In response, Triad lead chewed constantly into the walls and through the windows, zipping and ricochetting. Ki could hear Hyde and Queeg hurling directions and profanely demanding more action, while their crew moved in and about, seeking vulnerable points to strike.

Hastening back down the steep stairs, Ki returned to the barroom not a minute too soon, for Hyde had apparently deduced that only one gun was defending the front. And Queeg had ordered a charge. A dozen gunmen, sprinting hard across the clearing, were darting in for the protection of the porch and inset entryway. From his shooting angle, Napier couldn't get at them with his bullets. He yelled in alarm as he saw Ki unbarring the door. Then Ki was on his knees in the open doorway, triggering and levering as fast as he could.

The first gunman to come charging up the steps had his chest blasted and half his jaw knocked off. Another, peeping up, had his hat parted twice and flung himself at the ground. And the assaulting handful turned tail, retreating for cover at the edge of the clearing. When Ki rebarred the door he had blood staining the calf of one trouser leg, but he was chuckling calmly.

Jaw sagging, Napier handed Ki his kerchief.

"Only a scratch," Ki assured him, binding his leg with the kerchief. "Keep your nerve up. They got to do something soon."

"Maybe, maybe. But I wouldn't consider any of us in this place a good risk on a mortgage," Napier replied, sending slugs probing for the remaining Triad men.

The first rush was over. Enoch Hyde had undoubtedly been surprised at so much resistance. But Ki and Napier knew it wasn't the end by any means. A man devoid of the tiniest shred of humanity, Hyde craved the headband and Laverna either dead or a prisoner again, no matter the cost. And willing to get them for a price was Blackjack Queeg, a killer by instinct, who had utterly no regard for how much blood was spilled.

At back and front, crewmen drew off and ceased to attempt to charge. But from the scrub and boulders they kept sniping away with a sporadic yet lethal fire. Then, abruptly, there was silence, a hushed lull that contrasted eerily with the terrific din of moments before. Out of the stillness in back by the stable, Hyde shouted, "You, in there! Send Miss Pegaso out with the headband!"

Nobody inside answered immediately. Ki dashed to the rear window, where Laverna stood looking nervous and uncertain. "Nobody's sending you anywhere," he told her gently. Then he called out, "So you're playing it safe, eh, Hyde? Going back to your notion of marrying her so you'll be sure to own Triad, is that it? Well, I haven't the heart to send her to a fate worse'n death."

"It's your death if you don't! She comes with me, and I'll allow you hombres to ride away free."

"And you'll keep that bargain, Hyde?" Ki scoffed.

"What do you two mean to me? It's Triad I want. Or what's left of it, now that you've burned the ranch to the ground. All of Folgeron's precious trash and trinkets have gone up in smoke!"

"Gone!" Laverna gasped, brightening, then clutched Ki by the arm. "But that means you're

141

risking your lives over nothing. Listen, maybe I should go—"

"Not on our account," Ki said curtly. "Don't forget, Hyde is after the headband as well as you. He'd never believe we haven't got it. He'd figure we're holding out on him. Even if he did believe us, he'd still have us killed, either here or later on the trail. He'd be afraid we'd keep on hassling him, and anyway he can't afford to leave witnesses."

Impatiently Hyde yelled, "Well? Do we deal?"

Laverna gave Ki a long, troubled stare. Then she leaned out a little, so her voice would carry. "Mr. Hyde, I'd do deals with a mad dog before I'd do any kind of deal with you."

Most of the crewmen showed no expression in response to this whatever. But Blackjack Queeg began to pant. His arms jerked here and there, his eyes rolled spastically and his tongue flicked in and out, fluttering foam. Hyde's face darkened in stiff, clotted fury.

"Mad dog," he snarled. "I take that as a compliment."

If Hyde said anything more, it was lost in the suddenly renewed gunfire as Queeg signaled his gun crew back into action. Chunks of wall were bitten out as the cannonading fire sprayed bullets into the barroom. Front and back, the inn began to reek with cordite fumes and a fog of powder smoke began to thicken down from the ceiling.

If this wasn't a tight spot, then he'd never been caught in one, Ki was thinking as he returned fire. They had succeeded in thinning out this gun crew a little. But not enough. They were down to the last few boxes of ammunition and remained trapped in a house completely surrounded by vicious killers. Hyde and Queeg were still alive out yonder, urging on their men, yet careful of their own skins.

Well, the three of them might not weather this out, but they would certainly die trying. Not yet would Ki admit being whipped. Not while there still remained the slim chance of pulling a miracle out of nowhere. Swiftly he reloaded, his eyes constantly raking the clearing outside; then he flattened against the wall again as slugs coursed through the window.

"They're mounting another attack," he called in warning. "Here they come!"

★
Chapter 12

Jessica Starbuck had no idea that the Halfway Inn was under seige. Indeed, when she had ridden out at sunrise, leaving Laverna there to wait for Ki and Napier, her fear was that one or both of the men would never quit Triad range alive.

For a long stretch she followed the wagon trail at a swift pace. Her mount had rested a little, and despite the night's journey was in fine fettle. In fact, when you came right down to it, the pinto seemed in better shape than Jessie felt. Much of the way the trail crossed broad flatlands, sometimes three miles across with small mesas and pillars of wind-carved rocks rising from the floor. There also were side canyons, crooked and unexplored, every one of them a spot for ambush.

Nervous about riding so vulnerably exposed, Jessie left the trail and cut across some dry lake beds, rough from hoof marks pressed there the previous wet season, and swung through unmapped mesa and canyon with an eye to concealment. Presently she descended heaped talus rock at the face of a mesa toward the flyblown little town of Beyond.

Jogging into town, she listened carefully and gazed sharply at the structures lining the main street. Dusty, clad in range garb, her hair up under her hat and the brim tugged low, at a distance she could have been easily mistaken for a slim, young waddie, nobody in particular. Up close, of course, there was no foolin'. The few men loitering along the boardwalk gawked at her in slack-jawed astonishment, then proceeded to make themselves scarce. Running to fetch Otis Muell, she reckoned.

She was midway to the Ritz Hotel when the rifle sounded. The shot came from far enough away that the triggerman might have recognized her as a woman; or maybe he didn't care. And it passed so close to her that it might have been meant as a warning shot; or maybe he couldn't aim. Whichever, Jessie had no desire to wait and learn, and bailed out of her saddle. Letting her horse bolt, she lighted running, heading for the nearest doorway, which, by the very law of averages that prevailed in Beyond, happened to be the doorway of a saloon, called The Thundermug, to be exact.

Another rifle opened up, the gunfire scaring horses at hitch racks, starting a runaway here and there. But Jessie gained the bat wings unscathed and plunged inside furious and shaken. Startled, a bartender and three patrons gaped at her. Flourishing her pistol, Jessie snapped, "Out! All of you!" and herded them toward the back door. They went dazedly, stunned by the sudden entry of a woman into

145

the bar, and she prodded them through the door and locked it after them, then jammed a chair under the knob.

Returning to the front of the saloon, Jessie saw a half dozen men come charging along the street, headed by red-bearded Otis Muell. Jessie sprinkled a few bullets around their feet, discouraging them to the extent that they turned tail, scurrying across to the shelter of doorways and water troughs. Here they set up a barrage that blasted all the glass out of the front of the saloon and kept the bat wings swinging.

Jessie, crouching low, called: "Muell! Listen to me!"

"Just show y'self!" Muell shouted angrily. "That's all I ask, you cheap cutthroat! Just show y'self, an' I'll slice your ears off and feed yuh to the buzzards!"

"Muell, I've got something better to show you!"

The answer was another swarm of bullets, and Jessie began to grin in spite of herself as the irony of her dilemma struck her. She wanted to tell these dispossessed ranchers that they might have their land back, and she couldn't make herself heard over the thunder of their guns! But how could she silence them without risking a bloodbath . . . ?

The sight of splinters driven from the window by questing lead gave her a wild inspiration. Hunching low, she scuttled over behind the bar and helped herself to an armful of whiskey bottles, then crawled back and began setting them up on the windowsill, exposing no more than her hand. The next barrage smashed these bottles one by one.

"He loves me," Jessie intoned as the first bottle exploded. "He loves me not. He loves me. Not. Loves me. Not—"

She crept back for a second load of bottles, and when these fetched another volley, she heard an agonized wail across the street.

"Gawdaw'mighty, Otis! She's setting up all my stock to be smashed!" someone bleated, evidently the saloon's proprietor. "Lay off, will you, boys? Tell 'em to lay off, Otis! D'you want to shoot me outta business?"

There was an abrupt lull, broken only by Muell howling, "*She?* We been shootin' at a *she* in there?"

"Yeah, a female sportin' a gun!"

Muell snorted. "Scairt? Females can't shoot."

"I ain't hankerin' to test her," a third man complained. "She might go wavery and hit me by mistake, if she takes a notion to fire point-blank at you, Otis."

"He's right," another agreed. "Besides, it's tantamount to criminal to be spillin' good whiskey."

So far, so good, Jesse figured. She'd effected a deadlock of sorts, but she wasn't out there yet, with them listening to her instead of themselves. She couldn't show them the headband; it was packed in her saddlebag and not very convincing by itself. But the important part, the new will Folgeron had hidden under the sweat lining, had been removed back at the inn by her and Laverna, and was safely in her jacket pocket. She took it out now—a simple, single page, which had been folded to the width of a lamp wick to fit in the headband; it lacked the

147

"whereas"s' and other fancy lingo, but had a date, a signature, and was unquestionably handwritten by Folgeron. It was as legitimate as any of those Revengers grouped outside, and maybe more so.

On the floor by her hand lay one of the broken whiskey bottles. The neck had been sheared off, and the rotgut booze had drained out. Shaking the last few drops out, Jessie tucked the will into the bottle, then flung it out the window.

"Muell!" she called. "Have a look at the bottle!"

The bottle hit the far planking and rolled toward a doorway where one of the Revengers huddled. Jessie held her breath; would they suspect this was a ruse? An arm was gingerly extended; the bottle was snatched up. A minute passed, five . . .

"Jumpin' horny toads!" Muell suddenly bellowed. Another five minutes passed, then he shouted, "Lady! Miz Starbuck or whoever you is! If'n this is gen-uine, you oughta be willing to toss out your gun and come out with your hands hoisted!"

Immediately Jessie flung her pistol out through the broken window, onto the boardwalk, then walked through the bat wings with her hands raised. Men came converging from everywhere to form a close-packed circle around her. Otis Muell barged to the fore, scowling, the paper from the bottle in his hand.

"I'm supposed to swaller," he said skeptically, "that this's Folgeron's last testy-ment, and he intends to restitute our properties to us."

"Yes, and to give the Triad to Miss Pegaso, and his Indian collection to the government," Jessie confirmed. "It's my job to see that everybody gets what's due them, and I can't without your help. Believe me, if this will or Miss Pegaso fall into the hands of Folgeron's lawyer, Enoch Hyde, you can kiss your inheritances good-bye."

Muell glared suspiciously. "I think there's trickery here!"

"Oh, stop being so stupid!"

"It's too late for that now," he retorted, and turned to the Revengers. "Let's lock her in the storeroom again, till we check out her yarn."

"That coffin-toter's in there," a man reminded Muell. "And that one window is only boarded up. Mayhaps, 'twixt the two of 'em they'd bust out again."

"*Coffin*-toter?" Jessie queried.

"A freight hauling goods to Triad Ranch. We're holdin' him under grave suspicion, so to speak, and to plague Folgeron a mite. Folgeron can whistle Dixie for the fancy buryin'-box the freighter was fetchin' in."

"You won't bother Folgeron any," Jessie replied. "He's dead. Miss Pegaso can vouch for that, and I imagine that coffin is meant for him."

Muell blinked, scratched his beard. "Winthrop Folgeron dead? Say, now, p'raps you're telling us straight. The coffin fits in. Spill the rest of it."

Jessie sighed, impatient and frustrated. With lightning-quick phrases, she sketched the sequence of events as best she knew them up to this point, concluding, "Now look, Muell. I don't know if my friend Ki and Dutch Napier are trapped at Triad or made it to the inn, but I do know Laverna Pegaso

149

is waiting there for my return. She owns Triad now, knows it better than anyone alive, and wants to help you Revengers take control from Hyde. That's what you want, isn't it, a showdown? Well, here's your chance. Are you coming with me or not?"

A change came over the men like a cold wind blowing. They stared at each other, then at Muell, a question, almost a demand, in their grim eyes. Muell's forehead was pleated by the strain of hope and concern.

"B'gawd, it's our fight, too!" he declared suddenly. "I'm for it! Grab your weapons, plenty o' shells, and mount up, boys! We're ridin'!"

★

Chapter 13

"Here they come!" Ki warned, peering out the window.

Barely visible was Enoch Hyde, commanding from under cover of the stable, such an elegant target that he dared not participate in the frontal attack he was demanding. In the open stood Blackjack Queeg, disdaining even to crouch when bullets whipped close by. He wasn't doing any crowing, much less any giggling, yet his air of kill-thirsty confidence was infecting his gun crew, who were losing some of their newfound zeal at the sight of so many who'd plainly lost their lives.

More cautiously, but still urged on by Hyde, they swarmed toward the front and back doors, firing. One of the charging men stumbled, then another grabbed at a wounded arm as he slid downward. There were shrieks of pain, a wounded man's howl, as the three inside the inn covered the windows. One gunman, stocky and mustachioed, hesitated a moment before scrambling out from Napier's carbine sights. Two more followed, and the second attack was beaten back.

The odds had dropped. Blackjack Queeg's renegades had suffered a fierce toll, yet they were a callous and vicious lot who lived on the wages of blood, and heartbreak, and terror—and the trio they were up against had nothing but inflamed desperation. So this was not over, Ki reckoned; this was just another respite between skirmishes. He took advantage of the break to pass out the last boxes of ammunition, and happened to be up front with Napier when Laverna let out a scream. Both men rushed back to her, glancing out the window at where she was indicating.

Ki swore. "They got that old rusty wagon that was parked in the stable."

Pushing the ramshackle old hulk across the clearing, gunmen brought it to a halt about fifty yards away, at an angle to the building. The uplifted tongue of the wagon pointed at the rear door like a gaunt finger.

"Queeg's planning to do what you did to him," Napier said. "He's going to put some men in the wagon lying flat, and have the others roll it smack at us. We won't be able to pick 'em off in it. They'll smack into the door and . . ." He didn't want to go any further.

"Yes," Ki said grimly. Outside the men were shifting the wagon around to set it straight. "Guess we'll just have to fight them room to room."

"If we had lots of shells . . ." Laverna looked around, fingering her Bisley revolver. "Well, a brave woman dies only once; a wife to Hyde dies every night."

"I said we'd fight from room to room, Laverna," Ki stated, the fierce will behind his onyx eyes easing the cold despair that gnawed at her. "The wagon isn't going to climb the stairs. Now, you get upstairs with Dutch, and give them blazes when they try to get up there. Use your lead carefully and make them pay for each step."

Laverna crossed and started up, followed by Napier. He paused after a step to look back at Ki. "Aren't you coming?"

Ki smiled a little wearily. "I'm staying down here as a special . . . a special reception committee, you might say."

Napier and Laverna began to protest simultaneously. There was a bumping rumble from out in the clearing, the creaking groan of rusted wagon wheels stirring into motion. It jerked their heads around. Through the rear window the wagon could be seen gathering speed, like a juggernaut aiming to crush them once and for all . . .

Crouched behind the barroom counter, Ki could glimpse it hurtling toward the rear door. With the upraised tongue lashed to the front of the wagon, it stayed on its course, rocking when it hit stones but not swerving. Shoving from behind, with little more than arms, legs and hats visible, were most of Queeg's remaining crew. When they got closer, they began to slap lead at the inn to harry the defenders. The men flattened on the wagon bottom between the box and sideboards could not be seen at all.

Ki's hopes leapt as the wagon jounced over a rock and side-slipped off course. It slowed some, but headed for a point only a few feet from the rear doorway. Then luck swung with Triad. The wagon struck a pothole or rut and was deflected to hit the middle of the door. It came on like something in a nightmare, horseless, apparently without riders, gradually losing momentum. Slow, eternal seconds ticked off. Ki's eyes flicked over to the door to make doubly certain he had left it unlocked and unbarred. Then the wagon collided into the stoop as if aimed by a marksman, rebounding only a few feet. Before it had ceased motion, gunmen were piling out.

The stoop trembled under the pound of boots. The leading man opened the door and, crouched, swept his eyes around the bullet-spattered barroom. "Upstairs! The sonsabitches went upstairs! After 'em!" someone shouted.

Yelling, the first ones barged in, wheeling with cocked revolvers to make sure nobody was hidden in the powder smoke—dimmed recesses of the room. The one in the van, moving on legs thin as fence posts, ran for the stairs, tripping when his spur caught in a gash in the old carpet. A sawed-off breed flung past him and leapt up two, three steps. The next instant, he stopped as if he had slammed into an invisible wall.

From near the top of the stairs, muzzle flame had stabbed at him. And Laverna Pegaso's leather skirt was visible as she came down a couple of steps to get in the shot.

Blackjack Queeg's renegades, sensing the finish, didn't mean to be denied. They swarmed by the slowly spinning, dying breed, triggering. Dutch Napier's roar came from above. One of the charging men stumbled and clawed at his chest as he slid downward, step by step. There was a shriek of pain, a wounded man's cry, the assault up the staircase momentarily stalling.

"Burn 'em down!" Blackjack Queeg commanded, as more men stormed into the barroom. "Git every last one of 'em!"

A wounded gunman, worming out of the scramble, spotted Ki triggering as he straightened. He died in mid-scream. Two others swiveled. Their fire and that from Ki's carbine bridged the space between them and seemed to intermesh. Both buckled, gushing blood. But they had taken Ki's last two bullets.

A fourth man loomed up in front of the bar, aiming point-blank at Ki. Leaping over the counter, Ki whacked his empty carbine across the man's face and almost bent the barrel, the man falling away in a spew of teeth and blood. His place was instantly taken by another man, who leered as he strove to fire. The leer stayed put, but the head departed the body, for now Ki had drawn his *tanto* and was slashing the short, curve-bladed sword with precise strokes at bellies and limbs.

Even before the man's head hit the floor, Ki was swiveling, continuing the *tanto*'s arc to catch the next man, while lashing out with his slippered foot at a third. The third was flung swiftly back by Ki's smashing heel kick to his lower jaw. His jaw shattered and his throat ruptured; his call for help died stillborn. The second man had his mouth wide to yell but could not because his windpipe was severed, along with his jugular vein, which fountained blood as he toppled over.

Again Ki pivoted, peripherally glimpsing Blackjack Queeg centering a bead on him. But that third man, gasping, wheezing, doubling over in pain, was in the way and had to be dealt with first. Ki executed a forward somersault, rising in close and sliding his *tanto* into the man's belly, gutting up through his chest cavity.

Withdrawing his sword one-handed, Ki used his left hand to snag some *shuriken* out of his vest. As the gutted man collapsed in a gory heap, Blackjack Queeg took a clear shot, his revolver spitting flame. He was fast, but Ki was faster. A chunk of countertop splintered just by Ki's hip as he sprang sideward, back over the bar. Queeg jerked as though trying to re-aim, dead without knowing it. Three *shuriken* had struck him in a tight pattern, the first slicing deep where his heart should be, the second just above the bridge of his nose and the third in his larnyx. Blackjack Queeg began to crumple as though deflating and fired his revolver reflexively, blowing a hole in his foot.

Queeg's fall scarcely caused a ripple. The clash continued, a brutal mess, shots cracking, knives snicking, hands grappling for throats. There were probably not more than a dozen gunmen on their feet now, but they were mercenaries, and although Queeg was dead, their paymaster Hyde was still alive. Bitterness wrenched at Ki's face; it seemed as if he had lost the final play of the game.

Suddenly, far out on the wagon trail, a fresh burst of gunfire echoed faintly over the melee, and with it came the approaching rumble of horses' hoofs.

Somebody, somewhere, bawled, "The Revengers!"

Like a catalyst, it provoked a chain reaction. The gunmen faltered, milling for an instant, then began to retreat, ceasing their attempts to overrun the inn. The sound came nearer, and now Ki caught the hollow booming of those guns become a roar, and the rataplan of hoofbeats storming out front. The gunmen stampeded outside, opening fire again, but this time their shots were aimed toward the vanguard of riders pouring into the clearing. A moment afterward, the Halfway Inn yard was streaming with mounted men, shouting men, men swinging rifles and revolvers, men in blue jeans and checked shirts, men with battered chaps and stoved-in, big-brimmed hats.

Jessie was among the first to ride in, frantic with worry ever since she'd initially heard the sounds of battle here some distance away. Now her worst fears were realized, she saw as she galloped forward. Pandemonium gripped the inn's clearing. She heard bullets singing high and thin, and she caught the shrill outlandish yells of attackers and defenders alike embroiled in open combat. Dead men lay across doorways, under windows, around the grounds. Empty shells were littered everywhere, crunching underfoot. The air was overcast with pungent powder smoke, which was fuming so strongly

157

out of open windows that it appeared as if the interior of the inn was ablaze.

Abruptly her face took on a huge grin of astonished relief. Out of the rear door charged Ki, Laverna and Dutch Napier, shooting at Triad gunmen with weapons dropped by their dead comrades.

Responding, gunmen were throwing volley after volley at the trio and the Revengers bearing down on them, desperate to hurl them back. Enoch Hyde's raging voice was drowning the other shouts as he tried to establish authority, but the damage was done. Queeg's renegade gunmen were turning toward their horses, for even if Hyde was paymaster, they were reverting to habits common to hired killers: If at first you don't succeed, haul ass before it's shot off. And seeing he was being arbitrarily abandoned, Hyde swung after them.

"Cover me!" Jessie called, dismounting at a run.

Otis Muell and other nearby Revengers began concentrating methodically, implacably, on gunmen who were anywhere about her. And as the rest became aware of Jessie sprinting after Hyde, they joined in protectively, slamming lead at the scattering Triad crew.

Jessie lined out for the stable, seeing as she ran the low-crouched figure of Enoch Hyde swinging up on his mount near the wide doorway. The lawyer had one foot lifted to the stirrup and was trying to rise to the saddle when Jessie punched a shot at him. Hyde dropped back to the ground and made a half turn, a blank look on his face, then dove away as his horse reared off, and plunged into the concealing gloom of the stable.

Jessie charged the stable, while gunmen galloped past, beating a retreat as fast as they could spur, chased by Revengers. A man went down screaming; another fell back against the corral fence, striking the ground with his dead-solid weight. A slug blew a tiny geyser of dust at Jessie's feet; glass crashed somewhere as a shard of windowpane caved in.

Entering the stable, Jessie caught a glimpse of Hyde angling from one wall across toward the stalls. Apparently he spotted Jessie, for he took a quick side step, then flipped his revolver around and fired. Twice. It was shooting that sacrificed accuracy for rapidity. The first slug went singing emptily out the doorway behind her, a bad miss. The second slug tore through Jessie's upper sleeve. This one, the second one, had been the corrective shot, the target-finding shot of the hell-for-leather style of gunfighting, and it came too late.

For things had happened almost instantaneously between Hyde's two shots.

Hyde's second shot had been started by a man alive, and finished by a man dead.

Enoch Hyde, Jessie realized later when she thought it over, had meticulously done the thing he had trained himself to do, mixing skill with error, mixing the right way with the wrong way, mixing supposition with fact. The lunatic-wild shot part was okay, if you cared to gamble. But along with it, Hyde had followed some gunslick's bad advice. He had twisted his body sidewise. An old myth, surviving from dueling days, said this was the thing to do, that it presented a narrow target to your opponent. It was a narrower target, all right, but it lined up all your vitals conveniently for your opponent's bullet.

Jessie shot Hyde about eight inches below his armpit. Her powerful cartridge blasted its heavy slug through heart and lungs, and Hyde died on his feet.

Almost instantly, it seemed, a crowd assembled.

It formed a circle with an empty center, empty save for the dead attorney and Jessie standing thoughtfully over him, gazing down at him. No one, certainly not Otis Muell and his Revengers, seemed unhappy that Enoch Hyde was finished.

There was a tug at the back of Jessie's jacket, and she looked around to see Dutch Napier, agreeable, friendly, battle-scarred and exhausted.

He gave her a lopsided grin. "Saved by a woman."

She nodded, smiling wryly. "The great Henk Willem Adriannus Van der Napier, saved by a woman. Any complaints?"

"Nope," he said affably. "It's a mighty pleasant sensation."

★

Chapter 14

Some hours later, when the dead were buried and the wounded were patched and resting, Jessie, Ki, Napier and Laverna were gathered around a table in the shambles of the barroom. Relaxing, they ruminated over what had occurred, filling in one another on missing details.

At one point, Jessie turned to Laverna and asked, "After Folgeron died, why'd you stay on at Triad at all, knowing the likes of Enoch Hyde?"

"He threatened to publicize some pictures Winthrop had taken of me."

"What possible harm could that do?"

Laverna leaned close to Jessie and whispered in her ear. Jessie's eyes widened. Laverna whispered some more. Jessie gasped. "Mercy! What's this world coming to? Pornographic photographs!"

Demurely, Laverna said, "Not mine."

"No, surely not," Jessie hastened to assure her. "They're artistic poses of the classic nude form. Tastefully done, I'm sure."

"Not to my taste," Napier declared out of male orneriness.

Ki nodded, feeling a bit of the devil too. "I admit, I prefer my women without their appurtenances showing. They don't stay shaped without their stays on. If I have to look at naked females, I'm partial to Blackfeet gals, myself. Pretty, and sloe-eyed, and all hell and vinegar on a horse."

He ducked as a spittoon came sailing from where the ladies were seated. Picked up as the first thing handy, the spittoon was a dandy old crock, made of heavy brass with a lead-weighted bottom. It almost missed Ki.

Almost.

Watch for

LONE STAR AND THE RIVER PIRATES

107th novel in the exciting LONE STAR series
from Jove

Coming in July!

GILES TIPPETTE

Author of the best-selling WILSON YOUNG SERIES, BAD NEWS, and CROSS FIRE is back with his most exciting Western adventure yet!

JAILBREAK

Time is running out for Justa Williams, owner of the Half-Moon Ranch in West Texas. His brother Norris is being held in a Mexican jail, and neither bribes nor threats can free him.

Now, with the help of a dozen kill-crazy Mexican *banditos*, Justa aims to blast Norris out. But the worst is yet to come: a hundred-mile chase across the Mexican desert with fifty *federales* in hot pursuit.

The odds of reaching the Texas border are a million to nothing . . . and if the Williams brothers don't watch their backs, the road to freedom could turn into the road to hell!

"Turn the page for an exciting excerpt of. . . ."

JAILBREAK
by
Giles Tippette

On sale now, wherever Jove Books are sold!

At supper Norris, my middle brother, said, "I think we got some trouble on that five thousand acres down on the border near Laredo."

He said it serious, which is the way Norris generally says everything. I quit wrestling with the steak Buttercup, our cook, had turned into rawhide and said, "What are you talking about? How could we have trouble on land lying idle?"

He said, "I got word from town this afternoon that a telegram had come in from a friend of ours down there. He says we got some kind of squatters taking up residence on the place."

My youngest brother, Ben, put his fork down and said, incredulously, *"That* five thousand acres? Hell, it ain't nothing but rocks and cactus and sand. Why in hell would anyone want to squat on that worthless piece of nothing?"

Norris just shook his head. "I don't know. But that's what the telegram said. Came from Jack Cole. And if anyone ought to know what's going on down there it would be him."

I thought about it and it didn't make a bit of sense. I was Justa Williams, and my family, my two brothers and myself and our father, Howard, occupied a considerable ranch called the Half-Moon down along the Gulf of Mexico in Matagorda County, Texas. It was some of the best grazing land in the state and we had one of the best herds of purebred and crossbred cattle in that part of the country. In short we were pretty well-to-do.

But that didn't make us any the less ready to be stolen from, if indeed that was the case. The five thousand acres Norris had been talking about had come to us through a trade our father had made some years before. We'd never made any use of the land, mainly because, as Ben had said, it was pretty worthless and because it was a good two hundred miles from our ranch headquarters. On a few occasions we'd bought cattle in Mexico and then used the acreage to hold small groups on while we made up a herd. But other than that, it lay mainly forgotten.

I frowned. "Norris, this doesn't make a damn bit of sense. Right after supper send a man into Blessing with a return wire for Jack asking him if he's certain. What the hell kind of squatting could anybody be doing on that land?"

Ben said, "Maybe they're raisin' watermelons." He laughed.

I said, "They could raise melons, but there damn sure wouldn't be no water in them."

Norris said, "Well, it bears looking into." He got up, throwing his napkin on the table. "I'll go write out that telegram."

I watched him go, dressed, as always, in his town clothes. Norris was the businessman in the family. He'd been sent down to the University at Austin and had got considerable learning about the ins and outs of banking and land deals and all the other parts of our business that didn't directly involve the ranch. At the age of twenty-nine I'd been the boss of the operation a good deal longer than I cared to think about. It had been thrust upon me by our father when I wasn't much more than twenty. He'd said he'd wanted me to take over while he was still strong enough to help me out of my mistakes and I reckoned that was partly true. But it had just seemed that after our mother had died the life had sort of gone out of him. He'd been one of the earliest settlers, taking up the land not long after Texas had become a republic in 1845. I figured all the years of fighting Indians and then Yankees and scalawags and carpetbaggers and cattle thieves had taken their toll on him. Then a few years back he'd been nicked in the lungs by a bullet that should never have been allowed to head his way and it had thrown an extra strain on his heart. He was pushing seventy and he still had plenty of head on his shoulders, but mostly all he did now was sit around in his rocking chair and stare out over the cattle and land business he'd built. Not to say that I didn't go to him for advice when the occasion demanded. I did, and mostly I took it.

Buttercup came in just then and sat down at the end of the table with a cup of coffee. He was near as old as Dad and almost completely worthless. But he'd been one of the first hands that Dad had hired and he'd been kept on even after he couldn't sit a horse anymore. The problem was he'd elected himself cook, and that was the sorriest day our family had ever seen. There were two Mexican women hired to cook for the twelve riders we kept full time, but Buttercup insisted on cooking for the family.

Mainly, I think, because he thought he was one of the family. A notion we could never completely dissuade him from.

So he sat there, about two days of stubble on his face, looking as scrawny as a pecked-out rooster, sweat running down his face, his apron a mess. He said, wiping his forearm across his forehead, "Boy, it shore be hot in there. You boys shore better be glad you ain't got no business takes you in that kitchen."

Ben said, in a loud mutter, "I wish you didn't either."

Ben, at twenty-five, was easily the best man with a horse or a gun that I had ever seen. His only drawback was that he was hotheaded and he tended to act first and think later. That ain't a real good combination for someone that could go on the prod as fast as Ben. When I had argued with Dad about taking over as boss, suggesting instead that Norris, with his education, was a much better choice, Dad had simply said, "Yes, in some ways. But he can't handle Ben. You can. You can handle Norris, too. But none of them can handle you."

Well, that hadn't been exactly true. If Dad had wished it I would have taken orders from Norris even though he was two years younger than me. But the logic in Dad's line of thinking had been that the Half-Moon and our cattle business was the lodestone of all our businesses and only I could run that. He had been right. In the past I'd imported purebred Whiteface and Hereford cattle from up North, bred them to our native Longhorns and produced cattle that would bring twice as much at market as the horse-killing, all-bone, all-wild Longhorns. My neighbors had laughed at me at first, claiming those square little purebreds would never make it in our Texas heat. But they'd been wrong and, one by one, they'd followed the example of the Half-Moon.

Buttercup was setting up to take off on another one of his long-winded harangues about how it had been in the "old days" so I quickly got up, excusing myself, and went into the big office we used for sitting around in as well as a place of business. Norris was at the desk composing his telegram so I poured myself out a whiskey and sat down. I didn't want to hear about any trouble over some worthless five thousand acres of borderland. In fact, I didn't want to hear about any troubles of any kind. I was just two weeks short of getting married, married to a lady I'd been courting off and on for five years, and I was mighty anxious that nothing come up to interfere with our plans. Her name was Nora Parker and her daddy owned and run the general mercantile in our nearest town, Blessing. I'd almost lost her once before to a Kansas City drummer. She'd finally gotten tired of waiting on me, waiting until the ranch didn't occupy all my time, and almost run off with a smooth-talking Kansas City drummer that called on her daddy in the harness trade. But she'd come to her senses in time and got off the train in Texarkana and returned home.

But even then it had been a close thing. I, along with my men and brothers and help from some of our neighbors, had been involved with stopping a huge herd of illegal cattle being driven up from Mexico from crossing our range and infecting our cattle with tick fever which could have wiped us all out. I tell you it had been a bloody business. We'd lost four good men and had to kill at least a half dozen on the other side. Fact of the business was I'd come about as close as I ever had to getting killed myself, and that was going some for the sort of rough-and-tumble life I'd led.

Nora had almost quit me over it, saying she just couldn't take the uncertainty. But in the end, she'd stuck by me. That had been the year before, 1896, and I'd convinced her that civilized law was coming to the country, but until it did, we that had been there before might have to take things into our own hands from time to time.

She'd seen that and had understood. I loved her and she loved me and that was enough to overcome any of the troubles we were still likely to encounter from day to day.

So I was giving Norris a pretty sour look as he finished his telegram and sent for a hired hand to ride it into Blessing, seven miles away. I said, "Norris, let's don't make a big fuss about this. That land ain't even crossed my mind in at least a couple of years. Likely we got a few Mexican families squatting down there

172

and trying to scratch out a few acres of corn."

Norris gave me his businessman's look. He said, "It's our land, Justa. And if we allow anyone to squat on it for long enough or put up a fence they can lay claim. That's the law. My job is to see that we protect what we have, not give it away."

I sipped at my whiskey and studied Norris. In his town clothes he didn't look very impressive. He'd inherited more from our mother than from Dad so he was not as wide-shouldered and slim-hipped as Ben and me. But I knew him to be a good, strong, dependable man in any kind of fight. Of course he wasn't that good with a gun, but then Ben and I weren't all that good with books like he was. But I said, just to jolly him a bit, "Norris, I do believe you are running to suet. I may have to put you out with Ben working the horse herd and work a little of that fat off you."

Naturally it got his goat. Norris had always envied Ben and me a little. I was just over six foot and weighed right around a hundred and ninety. I had inherited my daddy's big hands and big shoulders. Ben was almost a copy of me except he was about a size smaller. Norris said, "I weigh the same as I have for the last five years. If it's any of your business."

I said, as if I was being serious, "Must be them sack suits you wear. What they do, pad them around the middle?"

He said, "Why don't you just go to hell."

After he'd stomped out of the room I got the bottle of whiskey and an extra glass and went down to Dad's room. It had been one of his bad days and he'd taken to bed right after lunch. Strictly speaking he wasn't supposed to have no whiskey, but I watered him down a shot every now and then and it didn't seem to do him no harm.

He was sitting up when I came in the room. I took a moment to fix him a little drink, using some water out of his pitcher, then handed him the glass and sat down in the easy chair by the bed. I told him what Norris had reported and asked what he thought.

He took a sip of his drink and shook his head. "Beats all I ever heard," he said. "I took that land in trade for a bad debt some fifteen, twenty years ago. I reckon I'd of been money ahead if I'd of hung on to the bad debt. That land won't even raise weeds, well as I remember, and Noah was in on the last rain that fell on the place."

We had considerable amounts of land spotted around the state as a result of this kind of trade or that. It was Norris's business to keep up with their management. I was just bringing this to Dad's attention more out of boredom and impatience for my wedding day to arrive than anything else.

I said, "Well, it's a mystery to me. How you feeling?"

He half smiled. "Old." Then he looked into his glass. "And I never liked watered whiskey. Pour me a dollop of the straight stuff in here."

I said, "Now, Howard. You know—"

He cut me off. "If I wanted somebody to argue with I'd send for Buttercup. Now do like I told you."

I did, but I felt guilty about it. He took the slug of whiskey down in one pull. Then he leaned his head back on the pillow and said, "Aaaaah. I don't give a damn what that horse doctor says, ain't nothing makes a man feel as good inside as a shot of the best."

I felt sorry for him laying there. He'd always led just the kind of life he wanted—going where he wanted, doing what he wanted, having what he set out to get. And now he was reduced to being a semi-invalid. But one thing that showed the strength that was still in him was that you *never* heard him complain. He said, "How's the cattle?"

I said, "They're doing all right, but I tell you we could do with a little of Noah's flood right now. All this heat and no rain is curing the grass off way ahead of time. If it doesn't let up we'll be feeding hay by late September, early October. And that will play hell on our supply. Could be we won't have enough to last through the winter. Norris thinks we ought to sell off five hundred head or so, but the market is doing poorly right now. I'd rather chance the weather than take a sure beating by selling off."

He sort of shrugged and closed his eyes. The whiskey was relaxing him. He said, "You're the boss."

"Yeah," I said. "Damn my luck."

I wandered out of the back of the house. Even though it was nearing seven o'clock of the evening it was still good and hot. Off in the distance, about a half a mile away, I could see the outline of the house I was building for Nora and myself. It was going to be a close thing to get it finished by our wedding day. Not having any riders to spare for the project, I'd imported a building contractor from Galveston, sixty miles away. He'd arrived with a half a dozen Mexican laborers and a few skilled masons and they'd set up a little tent city around the place. The contractor had gone back to Galveston to fetch more materials, leaving his Mexicans behind. I walked along idly, hoping he wouldn't forget that the job wasn't done. He had some of my money, but not near what he'd get when he finished the job.

Just then Ray Hays came hurrying across the back lot toward me. Ray was kind of a special case for me. The only problem with that was that he knew it and wasn't a bit above taking advantage of the situation. Once, a few years past, he'd saved my life by going against an evil man that he was working for at the time, an evil man who meant to have my life. In gratitude I'd given Ray a good job at the Half-Moon, letting him work directly under Ben, who was responsible for the horse herd. He was a good, steady man and a good man with a gun. He was also fair company. When he wasn't talking.

He came churning up to me, mopping his brow. He said, "Lordy, boss, it is—"

I said, "Hays, if you say it's hot I'm going to knock you down."

He gave me a look that was a mixture of astonishment and hurt. He said, "Why, whatever for?"

I said, "*Everybody* knows it's hot. Does every son of a bitch you run into have to make mention of the fact?"

His brow furrowed. "Well, I never thought of it that way. I 'spect you are right. Goin' down to look at yore house?"

I shook my head. "No. It makes me nervous to see how far they've got to go. I can't see any way it'll be ready on time."

He said, "Miss Nora ain't gonna like that."

I gave him a look. "I guess you felt forced to say that."

He looked down. "Well, maybe she won't mind."

I said, grimly, "The hell she won't. She'll think I did it a-purpose."

"Aw, she wouldn't."

"Naturally you know so much about it, Hays. Why don't you tell me a few other things about her."

"I was jest tryin' to lift yore spirits, boss."

I said, "You keep trying to lift my spirits and I'll put you on the haying crew."

He looked horrified. No real cowhand wanted any work he couldn't do from the back of his horse. Haying was a hot, hard, sweaty job done either afoot or from a wagon seat. We generally brought in contract Mexican labor to handle ours. But I'd been known in the past to discipline a cowhand by giving him a few days on the hay gang. Hays said, "Boss, now I never meant nothin'. I swear. You know me, my mouth gets to runnin' sometimes. I swear I'm gonna watch it."

I smiled. Hays always made me smile. He was so easily buffaloed. He had it soft at the Half-Moon and he knew it and didn't want to take any chances on losing a good thing.

I lit up a cigarillo and watched dusk settle in over the coastal plains. It wasn't but three miles to Matagorda Bay and it was quiet enough I felt like I could almost hear the waves breaking on the shore. Somewhere in the distance a mama cow bawled for her calf. The spring crop were near about weaned by now, but there were still a few mamas that wouldn't cut the apron strings. I stood there reflecting on how peaceful things had been of late. It suited me just fine. All I wanted was to get my house finished, marry Nora and never handle another gun so long as I lived.

The peace and quiet were short-lived. Within twenty-four hours we'd had a return telegram from Jack Cole. It said:

YOUR LAND OCCUPIED BY TEN TO TWELVE MEN STOP CAN'T BE SURE WHAT THEY'RE DOING BECAUSE THEY RUN STRANGERS OFF STOP APPEAR TO HAVE A GOOD MANY CATTLE GATHERED STOP APPEAR TO BE FENCING STOP ALL I KNOW STOP.

I read the telegram twice and then I said, "Why, this is crazy as hell! That land wouldn't support fifty head of cattle."

We were all gathered in the big office. Even Dad was there, sitting in his rocking chair. I looked up at him. "What do you make of this, Howard?"

He shook his big, old head of white hair. "Beats the hell out of me, Justa. I can't figure it."

Ben said, "Well, I don't see where it has to be figured. I'll take five men and go down there and run them off. I don't care what they're doing. They ain't got no business on our land."

I said, "Take it easy, Ben. Aside from the fact you don't need to be getting into any more fights this year, I can't spare you or five men. The way this grass is drying up we've got to keep drifting those cattle."

Norris said, "No, Ben is right. We can't have such affairs going on with our property. But we'll handle it within the law. I'll simply take the train down there, hire a good lawyer and have the matter settled by the sheriff. Shouldn't take but a few days."

Well, there wasn't much I could say to that. We couldn't very well let people take advantage of us, but I still hated to be without Norris's services even for a few days. On matters other than the ranch he was the expert, and it didn't seem like there was a day went by that some financial question didn't come up that only he could answer. I said, "Are you sure you can spare yourself for a few days?"

He thought for a moment and then nodded. "I don't see why not. I've just moved most of our available cash into short-term municipal bonds in Galveston. The market is looking all right and everything appears fine at the bank. I can't think of anything that might come up."

I said, "All right. But you just keep this in mind. You are not a gun hand. You are not a fighter. I do not want you going anywhere near those people, whoever they are. You do it legal and let the sheriff handle the eviction. Is that understood?"

He kind of swelled up, resenting the implication that he couldn't handle himself. The biggest trouble I'd had through the years when trouble had come up had been keeping Norris out of it. Why he couldn't just be content to be a wagon load of brains was more than I could understand. He said, "Didn't you just hear me say I intended to go through a lawyer and the sheriff? Didn't I just say that?"

I said, "I wanted to be sure you heard yourself."

He said, "Nothing wrong with my hearing. Nor my approach to this matter. You seem to constantly be taken with the idea that I'm always looking for a fight. I think you've got the wrong brother. I use logic."

"Yeah?" I said. "You remember when that guy kicked you in the balls when they were holding guns on us? And then we chased them twenty miles and finally caught them?"

He looked away. "That has nothing to do with this."

"Yeah?" I said, enjoying myself. "And here's this guy, shot all to hell. And what was it you insisted on doing?"

Ben laughed, but Norris wouldn't say anything.

I said, "Didn't you insist on us standing him up so you could kick him in the balls? Didn't you?"

He sort of growled, "Oh, go to hell."

I said, "I just want to know where the logic was in that."

He said, "Right is right. I was simply paying him back in kind. It was the only thing his kind could understand."

I said, "That's my point. You just don't go down there and go to paying back a bunch of rough hombres in kind. Or any other currency for that matter."

That made him look over at Dad. He said, "Dad,

will you make him quit treating me like I was ten years old? He does it on purpose."

But he'd appealed to the wrong man. Dad just threw his hands in the air and said, "Don't come to me with your troubles. I'm just a boarder around here. You get your orders from Justa. You know that."

Of course he didn't like that. Norris had always been a strong hand for the right and wrong of a matter. In fact, he may have been one of the most stubborn men I'd ever met. But he didn't say anything, just gave me a look and muttered something about hoping a mess came up at the bank while he was gone and then see how much boss I was.

But he didn't mean nothing by it. Like most families, we fought amongst ourselves and, like most families, God help the outsider who tried to interfere with one of us.

WESTERNS!

at least a savings of $3.00 each month below the publishers price. Second, there is never any shipping, handling or other hidden charges—Free home delivery. What's more there is no minimum number of books you must buy, you may return any selection for full credit and you can cancel your subscription at any time. A TRUE VALUE!

Mail the coupon below

To start your subscription and receive 2 FREE WESTERNS, fill out the coupon below and mail it today. We'll send your first shipment which includes 2 FREE BOOKS as soon as we receive it.

Mail To:
True Value Home Subscription Services, Inc.
P.O. Box 5235
120 Brighton Road
Clifton, New Jersey 07015-5235

10598

YES! I want to start receiving the very best Westerns being published today. Send me my first shipment of 6 Westerns for me to preview FREE for 10 days. If I decide to keep them, I'll pay for just 4 of the books at the low subscriber price of $2.45 each; a total of $9.80 (a $17.70 value). Then each month I'll receive the 6 newest and best Westerns to preview Free for 10 days. If I'm not satisfied I may return them within 10 days and owe nothing. Otherwise I'll be billed at the special low subscriber rate of $2.45 each; a total of $14.70 (at least a $17.70 value) and save $3.00 off the publishers price. There are never any shipping, handling or other hidden charges. I understand I am under no obligation to purchase any number of books and I can cancel my subscription at any time, no questions asked. In any case the 2 FREE books are mine to keep.

Name _____

Address _____ Apt. # _____

City _____ State_____ Zip _____

Telephone # _____

Signature _____
(if under 18 parent or guardian must sign)
Terms and prices subject to change.
Orders subject to acceptance by True Value Home Subscription Services, Inc.